The Elephant Man

A DRAMA

By Bernard Pomerance

Austin Community College
Learning Resources Center

SAMUEL FRENCH, INC.

25 West 45th Street   NEW YORK 10036
7623 Sunset Boulevard   HOLLYWOOD 90046
LONDON   *TORONTO*

INTRODUCTORY NOTE

The Elephant Man was suggested by the life of John Merrick, known as The Elephant Man. It is recounted by Sir Frederick Treves in *The Elephant Man and Other Reminiscences,* Cassell and Co. Ltd., 1923. This account is reprinted in *The Elephant Man, A Study in Human Dignity,* by Ashley Montagu, Ballantine Books, 1973, to whom much credit is due for reviving contemporary interest in the story. My own knowledge of it came via my brother Michael, who told me the story, provided me with xeroves of Treves' memoirs until I came on my own copy, and sent me the Montagu book. In Montagu's book are included photographs of Merrick as well as of Merrick's model of St. Phillip's Church. Merrick's bones are still at London Hospital.

I believe the building of the church model constitutes some kind of central metaphor, and the groping toward conditions where it can be built and the building of it are the action of the play. It does not, and should not, however, dominate the play visually, as I originally believed.

Merrick's face was so deformed he could not express any emotion at all. His speech was very difficult to understand without practice. Any attempt to reproduce his appearance and his speech naturalistically—*if* it were possible—would seem to me not only counterproductive, but, the more remarkably successful, the more distracting from the play. For how he appeared, let slide projections suffice.

If the pinheaded women are two actresses, then the play, in a pinch, can be performed with seven players, five men, two women.

The London production of *The Elephant Man* opened at the Hampstead Theatre, co-produced by the Hampstead Theatre and the Foco Novo Company, with the following cast:

CELLIST	Pat Arrowsmith
FREDERICK TREVES	David Allister
BELGIAN POLICEMAN	
CARR GOMM	William Hoyland
CONDUCTOR	
ROSS	Arthur Blake
BISHOP WALSHAM HOW	
SNORK	
JOHN MERRICK	David Schofield
PINHEAD	Judy Bridgland
NURSE SANDWICH	
PRINCESS ALEXANDRA	
DUCHESS	
JELLY WILLOW	
PINHEAD	Jennie Stoller
MRS. KENDAL	
COUNTESS	
PINHEAD MANAGER	Ken Drury
ENGLISH POLICEMAN	
PORTER	
LORD JOHN	
WILLOW	

This production was directed by Roland Rees; set and costumes by Tanya McCallin; costumes made and supervised by Lindy Hemming; lighting by Alan O'Toole; stage management by Clive Thacker, Neil Barnett, and Diana Goodman.

The Elephant Man was produced on Broadway at The Booth Theatre, on April 22, 1979, with the following cast:

FREDERICK TREVES	Kevin Conway
BELGIAN POLICEMAN	
CARR GOMM	Richard Clarke
CONDUCTOR	
ROSS	I. M. Hobson
BISHOP WALSHAM HOW	
SNORK	
JOHN MERRICK	Philip Anglim
PINHEAD MANAGER	John Neville-Andrews
LONDON POLICEMAN	
WILL	
EARL	
LORD JOHN	
PINHEAD	Cordis Heard
MISS SANDWICH	
COUNTESS	
PRINCESS ALEXANDRA	
MRS. KENDAL	Carole Shelley
PINHEAD	
ORDERLY	Dennis Creaghan
CELLIST	David Hess

This production was directed by Jack Hofsiss; set by David Jenkins; costumes by Julie Weiss; lighting by Beverly Emmons; produced by Richmond Crinkley, Elizabeth I. McCann, and Nelle Nugent; Ray Larsen and Ted Snowden, associate producers.

No one with any history of back trouble should attempt the part of MERRICK *as contorted. Anyone playing the part of* MERRICK *should be advised to consult a physician about the problems of sustaining any unnatural or twisted position.—B.P.*

CHARACTERS

FREDERICK TREVES, *a surgeon and teacher*
CARR GOMM, *administrator of the London Hospital*
ROSS, *Manager of the Elephant Man*
JOHN MERRICK, *the Elephant Man*
Three PINHEADS, *three women freaks whose heads are
        pointed*
BELGIAN POLICEMEN
LONDON POLICEMAN
MAN, *at a fairground in Brussels*
CONDUCTOR, *of Ostend-London boat train*
BISHOP WALSHAM HOW
PORTER, *at the London Hospital*
SNORK, *also a porter*
MRS. KENDAL, *an actress*
DUCHESS
COUNTESS
PRINCESS ALEXANDRA
LORD JOHN
NURSE, MISS SANDWICH

1884–1890. London. One scene is in Belgium.

MUSIC NOTE

Samuel French, Inc. can supply *amateurs* with a score for solo cello upon receipt of the following:

1.) $25.00 refundable deposit on return of the material in good condition.
2.) A $10.00 non-returnable rental fee.
3.) A music royalty fee of $10.00 for each performance planned, which must be paid for at the time of placing your order.
4.) $3.00 to cover postage and handling.

Production fees for stock performances quoted upon request.

Please be advised that Slides used in the original broadway production are handled by:

Chic Silber
Sunshine Scenic Studio
1501 Broadway Suite 2402
New York, N. Y. 10036

The Elephant Man

Scene 1

HE WILL HAVE 100 GUINEA
FEES BEFORE HE'S FORTY

The London Hospital, Whitechapel Rd. Enter Gomm,
enter Treves.

Treves. Mr. Carr Gomm? Frederick Treves. Your
new lecturer in anatomy.

Gomm. Age thirty-one. Books on Scrofula and Ap-
plied Surgical Anatomy—I'm happy to see you rising,
Mr. Treves. I like to see merit credited, and your
industry, accomplishment, and skill all do you credit.
Ignore the squalor of Whitechapel, the general dingi-
ness, neglect and poverty without, and you will find
a continual medical richesse in the London Hospital.
We study and treat the widest range of diseases and
disorders, and are certainly the greatest institution
of our kind in the world. The Empire provides un-
paralleled opportunities for our studies, as places
cruel to life are the most revealing scientifically. Add
to our reputation by going further, and that'll satisfy.
You've bought a house?

Treves. On Wimpole Street.

Gomm. Good. Keep at it, Treves. You'll have an
FRS and 100 guinea fees before you're forty. You'll
find it is an excellent consolation prize.

Treves. Consolation? I don't know what you mean.

Gomm. I know you don't. You will. (*Exits.*)

Treves. A happy childhood in Dorset.

A scientist in an age of science.

9

In an English age, an Englishman. A teacher and a doctor at the London. Two books published by my thirty-first year. A house. A wife who loves me, and my god, 100 guinea fees before I'm forty.

Consolation for what?

As of the year AD 1884, I, Freddie Treves, have excessive blessings. Or so it seems to me.

Blackout.

Scene 2

ART IS AS NOTHING TO NATURE

Whitechapel Rd. A storefront. A large advertisement of a creature with an elephant's head. Ross, *his manager.*

Ross. Tuppence only, step in and see: This side of the grave, John Merrick has no hope nor expectation of relief. In every sense his situation is desperate. His physical agony is exceeded only by his mental anguish, a despised creature without consolation. Tuppence only, step in and see! To live with his physical hideousness, incapacitating deformities and unremitting pain is trial enough, but to be exposed to the cruelly lacerating expressions of horror and disgust by all who behold him—is even more difficult to bear. Tuppence only, step in and see! For in order to survive, Merrick forces himself to suffer these humiliations, I repeat, humiliations, in order to survive, thus he exposes himself to crowds who pay to gape and yawp at this freak of nature, the Elephant Man.

(*Enter* TREVES *who looks at advertisement.*)

Ross. See Mother Nature uncorseted and in malignant rage! Tuppence.

TREVES. This sign's absurd. Half-elephant, half-man is not possible. Is he foreign?

Ross. Right, from Leicester. But noting to fear.

TREVES. I'm at the London across the road. I would be curious to see him if there is some genuine disorder. If he is a mass of papier-maché and paint however—

Ross. Then pay me nothing. Enter, sir. Merrick, stand up. Ya bloody donkey, up, up.

(*They go in, then emerge.* TREVES *pays.*)

TREVES. I must examine him further at the hospital. Here is my card. I'm Treves. I will have a cab pick him up and return him. My card will gain him admittance.

Ross. Five bob he's yours for the day.

TREVES. I wish to examine him in the interests of science, you see.

Ross. Sir, I'm Ross. I look out for him, get him his living. Found him in Leicester workhouse. His own ma put him there age of three. Couldn't bear the sight, well you can see why. We—he and I—are in business. He is our capital, see. Go to a bank. Go anywhere. Want to borrow capital, you pay interest. Scientists even. He's good value though. You won't find another like him.

TREVES. Fair enough. (*He pays.*)

Ross. Right. Out here, Merrick. Ya bloody donkey, out!

Lights fade out.

Scene 3

WHO HAS SEEN THE LIKE
OF THIS?

Treves lectures. Merrick contorts himself to approximate projected slides of the real Merrick.

Treves. The most striking feature about him was his enormous head. Its circumference was about that of a man's waist. From the brow there projected a huge bony mass like a loaf, while from the back of his head hung a bag of spongy fungous-looking skin, the surface of which was comparable to brown cauliflower. On the top of the skull were a few long lank hairs. The osseous growth on the forehead, at this stage about the size of a tangerine, almost occluded one eye. From the upper jaw there projected another mass of bone. It protruded from the mouth like a pink stump, turning the upper lip inside out, and making the mouth a wide slobbering aperture. The nose was merely a lump of flesh, only recognizable as a nose from its position. The deformities rendered the face utterly incapable of the expression of any emotion whatsoever. The back was horrible because from it hung, as far down as the middle of the thigh, huge sacklike masses of flesh covered by the same loathsome cauliflower stain. The right arm was of enormous size and shapeless. It suggested but was not elephantiasis, and was overgrown also with pendant masses of the same cauliflower-like skin. The right hand was large and clumsy—a fin or paddle rather than a hand. No distinction existed between the palm and back, the thumb was like a radish, the fingers like thick tuberous roots. As a limb it was useless. The other arm was remarkable by contrast.

It was not only normal, but was moreover a delicately shaped limb covered with a fine skin and provided with a beautiful hand which any woman might have envied. From the chest hung a bag of the same repulsive flesh. It was like a dewlap suspended from the neck of a lizard. The lower limbs had the characters of the deformed arm. They were unwieldy, dropsical-looking, and grossly misshapen. There arose from the fungous skin growths a very sickening stench which was hard to tolerate. To add a further burden to his trouble, the wretched man when a boy developed hip disease which left him permanently lame, so that he could only walk with a stick. (*To* MERRICK.) Please. (MERRICK *walks.*) He was thus denied all means of escape from his tormentors.

VOICE. Mr. Treves, you have shown a profound and unknown disorder to us. You have said when he leaves here it is for his exhibition again. I do not think it ought to be permitted. It is a disgrace. It is a pity and a disgrace. It is an indecency in fact. It may be a danger in ways we do not know. Something ought to be done about it.

TREVES. I am a doctor. What would you have me do?

VOICE. Well. I know what to do. *I* know.

Silence. A policeman enters as lights fade out.

SCENE 4

THIS INDECENCY MAY NOT CONTINUE

Music. A fair. PINHEADS *huddling together, holding a portrait of Leopold, King of the Congo. Enter* MAN.

MAN. Now my pinheaded darlings, your attention please. Every freak in Brussels Fair is doing something to celebrate Leopold's fifth year as King of the Congo. Him. Our King. Our Empire. (*They begin reciting.*) No, don't recite yet, you morons. I'll say when. And when you do, get it *right*. You don't, it's back to the asylum. Know what that means, don't you? They'll cut your heads. They'll spoon out your little brains, replace 'em in the dachshund they were nicked from. *Cut you.* Yeah. Be back with customers. Come see the Queens of the Congo! (*Exits.*)

(*Enter* MERRICK, ROSS.)

MERRICK. Cosmos? Cosmos?

ROSS. Congo. Land of darkness. Hoho! (*See* PINS.) Look at them, lad. It's freer on the continent. Loads of indecency here, no one minds. You won't get coppers sent round to roust you out like London. Reckon in Brussels here's our fortune. You have a little tête-à-tête with this lot while I see the coppers about our license to exhibit. Be right back. (*Exits.*)

MERRICK. I come from England.

PINS. Allo!

MERRICK. At home they chased us. Out of London. Police. Someone complained. They beat me. You have no trouble? No?

PINS. Allo! Allo!

MERRICK. Hello. In Belgium we make money. I look forward to it. Happiness, I mean. You pay your police? How is it done?

PINS. Allo! Allo!

MERRICK. We do a show together sometime? Yes? I have saved forty-eight pounds. Two shillings. Nine pence. English money. Ross takes care of it.

PINS. Allo! Allo!

MERRICK. Little vocabulary problem, eh? Poor things. Looks like they put your noses to the grindstone and forgot to take them away.

(MAN *enters*.)

MAN. They're coming. (*People enter to see the girls' act.*) Now.

PINS. (*Dancing and singing*):

> Wo are the Queens of the Congo,
> The Beautiful Belgian Empire
> Our niggers are bigger
> Our miners are finer
> Empire, Empire, Congo and power
> Civilizuzu's finest hour
> Admire, perspire, desire, acquire
> Or we'll set you on fire!

MAN. You cretins! Sorry, they're not ready yet. Out please. (*People exit.*) Get those words right, girls! Or you know what. (MAN *exits*. PINS *weep*.)

MERRICK. Don't cry. You sang nicely. Don't cry. There there.

(*Enter* Ross *in grip of two* POLICEMEN.)

Ross. I was promised a permit. I lined a tour up on that!

POLICEMEN. This is a brutal, indecent, and immoral display. It is a public indecency, and it is forbidden here.

Ross. What about them with their perfect cone heads?

POLICEMEN. They are ours.

ROSS. Competition's good for business. Where's your spirit of competition?

POLICEMEN. Right here. (*Smacks* MERRICK.)

ROSS. Don't do that, you'll kill him!

POLICEMEN. Be better off dead. Indecent bastard.

MERRICK. Don't cry girls. Doesn't hurt.

PINS. Indecent, indecent, indecent, indecent!!

(POLICEMEN *escort* MERRICK *and* ROSS *out, i.e., forward. Blackout except spot on* MERRICK *and* ROSS.

MERRICK. Ostend will always mean bad memories. Won't it, Ross?

ROSS. I've decided. I'm sending you back, lad. You're a flop. No, you're a liability. You ain't the moneymaker I figured, so that's it.

MERRICK. Alone?

ROSS. Here's a few bob, have a nosh. I'm keeping the rest. For my trouble. I deserve it, I reckon. Invested enough with you. Pick up your stink if I stick around. Stink of failure. Stink of lost years. Just stink, stink, stink, stink, stink.

(*Enter* CONDUCTOR.)

CONDUCTOR. This the one?

ROSS. Just see him to Liverpool St. Station safe, will you? Here's for your trouble.

MERRICK. Robbed.

CONDUCTOR. What's he say?

ROSS. Just makes sounds. Fella's an imbecile.

MERRICK. Robbed.

Ross. Bon voyage, Johnny. His name is Johnny. He knows his name, that's all, though.

CONDUCTOR. Don't follow him, Johnny. Johnny, come on boat now. Conductor find Johnny place out of sight. Johnny! Johnny! Don't struggle, Johnny. Johnny come on.

MERRICK. Robbed! Robbed!

Fadeout on struggle.

SCENE 5

POLICE SIDE WITH IMBECILE AGAINST THE CROWD

Darkness. Uproar, shouts.

VOICE. Liverpool St. Station!

(*Enter* MERRICK, CONDUCTOR, POLICEMAN.)

POLICEMAN. We're safe in here. I barred the door.

CONDUCTOR. They wanted to rip him to pieces. I've never seen anything like it. It was like being Gordon at bleedin' Khartoum.

POLICEMAN. Got somewhere to go in London, lad? Can't stay here.

CONDUCTOR. He's an imbecile. He don't understand. Search him.

POLICEMAN. Got any money?

MERRICK. Robbed.

POLICEMAN. What's that?

CONDUCTOR. He just makes sounds. Frightened sounds is all he makes. Go through his coat.

MERRICK. Je-sus.

POLICEMAN. Don't let me go through your coat, I'll turn you over to that lot! Oh, I was joking, don't upset yourself.

MERRICK. Joke? Joke?

POLICEMAN. Sure, croak, croak, croak, croak.

MERRICK. Je-sus.

POLICEMAN. Got a card here. You Johnny Merrick? What's this old card here, Johnny? Someone give you a card?

CONDUCTOR. What's it say?

POLICEMAN. Says Mr. Frederick Treves, Lecturer in Anatomy, the London Hospital.

CONDUCTOR. I'll go see if I can find him, it's not far. (*Exits.*)

POLICEMAN. What's he do, lecture you on your anatomy? People who think right don't look like that then, do they? Yeah, glung glung, glung, glung.

MERRICK. Jesus. Jesus.

POLICEMAN. Sure, Treves, Treves, Treves, Treves.

(*Blackout, then lights go up as* CONDUCTOR *leads* TREVES *in.*)

TREVES. What is going on here? Look at that mob, have you no sense of decency. I am Frederick Treves. This is my card.

POLICEMAN. This poor wretch here had it. Arrived from Ostend.

TREVES. Good Lord, Merrick? John Merrick? What has happened to you?

MERRICK. Help me!

Fadeout.

SCENE 6

EVEN ON THE NIGER AND CEYLON, NOT THIS

The London Hospital. MERRICK *in bathtub.* TREVES *outside. Enter* MISS SANDWICH.

TREVES. You are? Miss Sandwich?

SANDWICH. Sandwich. Yes.

TREVES. You have had experience in missionary hospitals in the Niger

SANDWICH. And Ceylon.

TREVES. I may assume you've seen—

SANDWICH. The tropics. Oh those diseases. The many and the awful scourges our Lord sends, yes, sir.

TREVES. I need the help of an experienced nurse, you see.

SANDWICH. Someone to bring him food, take care of the room. Yes, I understand. But it is somehow difficult.

TREVES. Well, I have been let down so far. He really is—that is, the regular sisters—well, it is not part of their job and they will not do it. Be ordinarily kind to Mr. Merrick. Without—well—panicking. He is quite beyond ugly. You understand that? His appearance has terrified them.

SANDWICH. The photographs show a terrible disease.

TREVES. It is a disorder, not a disease; it is in no way contagious though we don't in fact know what it is. I have found however that there is a deep superstition in those I've tried, they actually believe he somehow brought it on himself, this thing, and of course it is not that at all.

SANDWICH. I am not one who believes it is ourselves who attain grace or bring chastisement to us, sir.

TREVES. Miss Sandwich, I am hoping not.

SANDWICH. Let me put your mind to rest. Care for lepers in the East, and you have cared, Mr. Treves. In Africa, I have seen dreadful scourges quite unknown to our more civilized climes. What at home could be worse than a miserable and afflicted rotting black?

TREVES. I imagine.

SANDWICH. Appearances do not daunt me.

TREVES. It is really that that has sent me outside the confines of the London seeking help.

SANDWICH. "I look unto the hills whence cometh my help." I understand: I think I will be satisfactory.

(Enter PORTER *with tray.)*

PORTER. His lunch. *(Exits.)*

TREVES. Perhaps you would be so kind as to accompany me this time. I will introduce you.

SANDWICH. Allow me to carry the tray.

TREVES. I will this time. You are ready.

SANDWICH. I am.

TREVES. He is bathing to be rid of his odor. *(They enter to* MERRICK.*)* John, this is Miss Sandwich. She—

SANDWICH. I— *(Unable to control hereself.)* Oh my good God in heaven. *(Bolts room.)*

TREVES. *(Puts* MERRICK's *lunch down.)* I am sorry. I thought—

MERRICK. Thank you for saving the lunch this time.

TREVES. Excuse me. *(Exits to* MISS SANDWICH.*)* You have let me down, you know. I did everything to warn you and still you let me down.

SANDWICH. You didn't say.

TREVES. But I—

SANDWICH. Didn't! You said—just words!

TREVES. But the photographs.

SANDWICH. Just pictures. No one will do this. I am sorry. (*Exits.*)

TREVES. Yes. Well. This is not helping him.

Fadeout.

SCENE 7

THE ENGLISH PUBLIC WILL PAY FOR HIM TO BE LIKE US

The London Hospital. MERRICK *in a bathtub reading.* TREVES, BISHOP How *in foreground.*

BISHOP. With what fortitude he bears his cross! It is remarkable. He has made the acquaintance of religion and knows sections of the Bible by heart. Once I'd grasped his speech, it became clear he'd certainly had religious instruction at one time.

TREVES. I believe it was in the workhouse, Dr. How.

BISHOP. They are awfully good about that sometimes. The psalms he loves, and the book of Job perplexes him, he says, for he cannot see that a just God must cause suffering, as he puts it, merely then to be merciful. Yet that Christ will save him he does not doubt, so he is not resentful.

(*Enter* GOMM.)

GOMM. Christ had better; be dammed if we can.

BISHOP. Ahem. In any case Dr. Treves, he has a

religious nature, further instruction would uplift him and I'd be pleased to provide it. I plan to speak of him from the pulpit this week.

GOMM. I see our visiting bather has flushed the busy Bishop How from his cruciform lair.

BISHOP. Speak with Merrick, sir. I have spoken to him of Mercy and Justice. There's a true Christian in the rough.

GOMM. This makes my news seem banal, yet: Frederick, the response to my letter to the *Times* about Merrick has been staggering. The English public has been so generous that Merrick may be supported for life without a penny spent from Hospital funds.

TREVES. But that is excellent.

BISHOP. God bless the English public.

GOMM. Especially for not dismembering him at Liverpool St. Station. Freddie, the London's no home for incurables, this is quite irregular, but for you I permit it—though god knows what you'll do.

BISHOP. God does know, sir, and Darwin does not.

GOMM. He'd better, sir; he deformed him.

BISHOP. I had apprehensions coming here. I find it most fortunate Merrick is in the hands of Dr. Treves, a Christian, sir.

GOMM. Freddie is a good man and a brilliant doctor, and that is fortunate indeed.

TREVES. I couldn't have raised the funds though, Doctor.

BISHOP. Don't let me keep you longer from your duties, Mr. Treves. Yet, Mr. Gomm, consider: is it science, sir, that motivates us when we transport English rule of law to India or Ireland? When good British churchmen leave hearth and home for missionary hardship in Africa, is it science that bears them away? Sir it is not. It is Christian duty. It is the obligation to bring our light and benefices to benighted man. That motivates us, even as it motivates Treves toward Merrick, sir, to bring salvation where none is. Gordon was a Christian, sir, and died at Khartoum for it. Not for science, sir.

GOMM. You're telling me, not for science.

BISHOP. Mr. Treves, I'll visit Merrick weekly if I may.

TREVES. You will be welcome, sir, I am certain.

BISHOP. Then good day, sirs. (*Exits.*)

GOMM. Well, Jesus my boy, now we have the money, what do you plan for Merrick?

TREVES. Normality as far as is possible.

GOMM. So he will be like us? Ah. (*Smiles.*)

TREVES. Is something wrong, Mr. Gomm? With us?

Fadeout.

SCENE 8

MERCY AND JUSTICE ELUDE OUR MINDS AND ACTIONS

MERRICK *in bath.* TREVES, GOMM.

MERRICK. How long is as long as I like?

TREVES. You may stay for life. The funds exist.

MERRICK. Been reading this. About homes for the blind. Wouldn't mind going to one when I have to move.

TREVES. But you do not have to move; and you're not blind.

MERRICK. I would prefer it where no one stared at me.

GOMM. No one will bother you here.

TREVES. Certainly not. I've given instructions.

(PORTER *and* SNORK *peek in.*)

PORTER. What'd I tell you?

SNORK. Gawd almighty. Oh. Mr. Treves. Mr. Gomm.

TREVES. You were told not to do this. I don't understand. You must not lurk about. Surely you have work.

PORTER. Yes, sir.

TREVES. Well, it is infuriating. When you are told a thing, you must listen. I won't have you gaping in on my patients. Kindly remember that.

PORTER. Isn't a patient, sir, is he?

TREVES. Do not let me find you here again.

PORTER. Didn't know you were here, sir. We'll be off now.

GOMM. No, no, Will. Mr. Treves was precisely saying no one would intrude when you intruded.

TREVES. He is warned now. Merrick does not like it.

GOMM. He was warned before. On what penalty, Will?

PORTER. That you'd sack me, sir.

GOMM. You are sacked, Will. You, his friend, you work here?

SNORK. Just started last week, sir.

GOMM. Well, I hope the point is taken now.

PORTER. Mr. Gomm—I ain't truly sacked, am I?

GOMM. Will, yes. Truly sacked. You will never be more truly sacked.

PORTER. It's not me. My wife ain't well. My sister has got to take care of our kids, and of her. Well.

GOMM. Think of them first next time.

PORTER. It ain't as if I interfered with his medicine.

GOMM. That is exactly what it is. You may go.

PORTER. Just keeping him to look at in private. That's all. Isn't it?

(SNORK *and* PORTER *exit.*)

GOMM. There are priorities, Frederick. The first is discipline. Smooth is the passage to the tight ship's master. Merrick, you are safe from prying now.

TREVES. Have we nothing to say, John?

MERRICK. If all that'd stared at me'd been sacked—there'd be whole towns out of work.

TREVES. I meant, "Thank you, sir."

MERRICK. "Thank you sir."

TREVES. We always do say please and thank you, don't we?

MERRICK. Yes, sir. Thank you.

TREVES. If we want to properly be like others.

MERRICK. Yes, sir, I want to.

TREVES. Then it is for our own good, is it not?

MERRICK. Yes, sir. Thank you, Mr. Gomm.

GOMM. Sir, you are welcome. (*Exits.*)

TREVES. You are happy here, are you not, John?

MERRICK. Yes.

TREVES. The baths have rid you of the odor, have they not?

MERRICK. First chance I had to bathe regular. Ly.

TREVES. And three meals a day delivered to your room?

MERRICK. Yes, sir.

TREVES. This is your Promised Land is it not? A roof. Food. Protection. Care. Is it not?

MERRICK. Right, Mr. Treves.

TREVES. I will bet you don't know what to call this.

MERRICK. No, sir, I don't know.

TREVES. You call it, Home.

MERRICK. Never had a home before.

TREVES. You have one now. Say it, John: Home.

MERRICK. Home.

TREVES. No, no, really say it. I have a home. This is my. Go on.

MERRICK. I have a home. This is my home. This is my home. I have a home. As long as I like?

TREVES. That is what home is.

MERRICK. That is what is home.

TREVES. If I abide by the rules, I will be happy.

MERRICK. Yes, sir.

TREVES. Don't be shy.

MERRICK. If I abide by the rules I will be happy.

TREVES. Very good. Why?

MERRICK. Why what?

TREVES. Will you be happy?

MERRICK. Because it is my home?

TREVES. No, no. Why do rules make you happy?

MERRICK. I don't know.

TREVES. Of course you do.

MERRICK. No, I really don't.

TREVES. Why does anything make you happy?

MERRICK. Like what? Like what?

TREVES. Don't be upset. Rules make us happy because they are for our own good.

MERRICK. Okay.

TREVES. Don't be shy, John. You can say it.

MERRICK. This is my home?

TREVES. No. About rules making us happy.

MERRICK. They make us happy because they are for our own good.

TREVES. Excellent. Now: I am submitting a follow-up paper on you to the London Pathological Society.

It would help if you told me what you recall about
your first years, John, To fill in gaps.

MERRICK. To fill in gaps. The workhouse where they
put me. They beat you there like a drum. Boom
boom: scrape the floor white. Shine the pan, boom
boom. It never ends. The floor is always dirty. The
pan is always tarnished. There is nothing you can do
about it. You are always attacked anyway. Boom
boom. Boom boom. Boom boom. Will the children go
to the workhouse?

TREVES. What children?

MERRICK. The children. The man he sacked.

TREVES. Of necessity. Will will find other employ-
ment. You don't want crowds staring at you, do you?

MERRICK. No.

TREVES. In your own home you do not have to have
crowds staring at you. Or anyone. Do you? In your
home?

MERRICK. No.

TREVES. Then Mr. Gomm was merciful. You yourself are proof. Is it not so? (*Pause.*) Well? Is it not
so?

MERRICK. If your mercy is so cruel, what do you
have for justice?

TREVES. I am sorry. It is just the way things are.

MERRICK. Boom boom. Boom boom. Boom boom.

Fadeout.

SCENE 9

MOST IMPORTANT ARE WOMEN

MERRICK *asleep, head on knees.* TREVES, MRS. KEN-
DAL *foreground.*

TREVES. You have seen photographs of John Merrick, Mrs. Kendal. You are acquainted with his appearance.

MRS. KENDAL. He reminds me of an audience I played Cleopatra for in Brighton once. All huge grim head and grimace and utterly unable to clap.

TREVES. Well. My aim's to lead him to as normal a life as possible. His terror of us all comes from having been held at arm's length from society. I am determined that shall end. For example, he loves to meet people and converse. I am determined he shall. For example, he had never seen the inside of any normal home before. I had him to mine, and what a reward, Mrs. Kendal; his astonishment, his joy at the most ordinary things. Most critical I feel, however, are women. I will explain. They have always shown the greatest fear and loathing of him. While he adores them of course.

MRS. KENDAL. Ah. He is intelligent.

TREVES. I am convinced they are the key to retrieving him from his exclusion. Though, I must warn you, women are not quite real to him—more creatures of his imagination.

MRS. KENDAL. Then he is already like other men, Mr. Treves.

TREVES. So I thought, an actress could help. I mean, unlike most women, you won't give in, you are trained to hide your true feelings and assume others.

MRS. KENDAL. You mean unlike most women I am famous for it, that is really all.

TREVES. Well. In any case. If you could enter the room and smile and wish him good morning. And when you leave, shake his hand, the left one is usable, and really quite beautiful, and say, "I am very pleased to have made your acquaintance, Mr. Merrick."

MRS. KENDAL. Shall we try it? Left hand out please. (*Suddenly radiant.*) I am *very* pleased to have made your made your acquaintance Mr. Merrick. I am very *pleased* to have made your acquaintance Mr. Merrick. I am very pleased to have made your *acquaintance* Mr. Merrick. I *am* very pleased to have made *your* acquaintance Mr. Merrick. Yes. That one.

TREVES. By god, they are all splendid. Merrick will be so pleased. It will be the day he becomes a man like other men.

MRS. KENDAL. Speaking of that, Mr. Treves.

TREVES. Frederick, please.

MRS. KENDAL. Freddie, may I commit an indiscretion?

TREVES. Yes?

MRS. KENDAL. I could not but help noticing from the photographs that—well—of the unafflicted parts— ah, how shall I put it? (*Points to photograph.*)

TREVES. Oh. I see! I quite. Understand. No, no, no, it is quite normal.

MRS. KENDAL. I thought as much.

TREVES. Medically speaking, uhm, you see the papillomatous extrusions which disfigure him, uhm, seem to correspond quite regularly to the osseous deformities, that is, excuse me, there is a link between the bone disorder and the skin growths, though for the life of me I have not discovered what it is or why it is, but in any case this—part—it would be therefore unlikely to be afflicted because well, that is, well, there's no bone in it. None in it. None at all. I mean.

MRS. KENDAL. Well. Learn a little every day don't we?

TREVES. I am horribly embarrassed.

MRS. KENDAL. Are you? Then he must be lonely indeed.

Fadeout.

S<small>CENE</small> 10

WHEN THE ILLUSION ENDS HE
MUST KILL HIMSELF

M<small>ERRICK</small> *sketching. Enter* T<small>REVES</small>, M<small>RS.</small> K<small>ENDAL</small>.

T<small>REVES</small>. He is making sketches for a model of St. Phillip's church. He wants someday to make a model, you see. John, my boy, this is Mrs. Kendal. She would very much like to make your acquaintance.

M<small>RS.</small> K<small>ENDAL</small>. Good morning Mr. Merrick.

T<small>REVES</small>. I will see to a few matters. I will be back soon. (*Exits.*)

M<small>ERRICK</small>. I planned so many things to say. I forget them. You are so beautiful.

M<small>RS.</small> K<small>ENDAL</small>. Good morning Mr. Merrick.

M<small>ERRICK</small>. Well. Really that was what I planned to say. That I forgot what I planned to say. I couldn't think of anything else I was so excited.

M<small>RS.</small> K<small>ENDAL</small>. Real charm is always planned, don't you think?

M<small>ERRICK</small>. Well. I do not know why I look like this, Mrs. Kendal. My mother was so beautiful. She was knocked down by an elephant in a circus while she was pregnant. Something must have happened, don't you think?

M<small>RS.</small> K<small>ENDAL</small>. It may well have.

M<small>ERRICK</small>. It may well have. But sometimes I think my head is so big because it is so full of dreams. Because it is. Do you know what happens when dreams cannot get out?

M<small>RS.</small> K<small>ENDAL</small>. Why no.

M<small>ERRICK</small>. I don't either. Something must. (*Silence.*) Well, You are a famous actress.

MRS. KENDAL. I am not unknown.

MERRICK. You must display yourself for your living then. Like I did.

MRS. KENDAL. That is not myself, Mr. Merrick. That is an illusion. This is myself.

MERRICK. This is myself too.

MRS. KENDAL. Frederick says you like to read. So: books.

MERRICK. I am reading *Romeo and Juliet* now.

MRS. KENDAL. Ah. Juliet. What a love story. I adore love stories.

MERRICK. I like love stories best too. If I had been Romeo, guess what.

MRS. KENDAL. What?

MERRICK. I would not have held the mirror to her breath.

MRS. KENDAL. You mean the scene where Juliet appears to be dead and he holds a mirror to her breath and sees—

MERRICK. Nothing. How does it feel when he kills himself because he just sees nothing?

MRS. KENDAL. Well. My experience as Juliet has been—particularly with an actor I will not name—that while I'm laying there dead dead dead, and he is lamenting excessively, I get to thinking that if this slab of ham does not part from the hamhock of his life toute suite, I am going to scream, pop off the tomb, and plunge a dagger into his scene-stealing heart. Romeos are very undependable.

MERRICK. Because he does not care for Juliet.

MRS. KENDAL. Not care?

MERRICK. Does he take her pulse? Does he get a doctor? Does he make sure? No. He kills himself. The illusion fools him because he does not care for her.

He only cares for himself. If I had been Romeo, we would have got away.

MRS. KENDAL. But then there would be no play, Mr. Merrick.

MERRICK. If he did not love her, why should there be a play? Looking in a mirror and seeing nothing. That is not love. It was an illusion. When the illusion ended he had to kill himself.

MRS. KENDAL. Why. That is extraordinary.

MERRICK. Before I spoke with people, I did not think of all these things because there was no one to bother to think them for. Now things just come out of my mouth which are true.

(TREVES *enters.*)

TREVES. You are famous, John. We are in the papers. Look. They have written up my report to the Pathological Society. Look—it is a kind of apotheosis for you.

MRS. KENDAL. Frederick, I feel Mr. Merrick would benefit by even more company than you provide; in fact by being acquainted with then best, and they with him. I shall make it my task if you'll permit. As you know, I am a friend of nearly everyone, and I do pretty well as I please and what pleases me is this task, I think.

TREVES. By god, Mrs. Kendal, you are splendid.

MRS. KENDAL. Mr. Merrick I must go now. I should like to return if I may. And so that we may without delay teach you about society, I would like to bring my good friend Dorothy Lady Neville. She would be most pleased if she could meet you. Let me tell her yes? (MERRICK *nods yes.*) Then until next time. I'm sure your church model will surprise us all. Mr. Merrick, it has been a very great pleasure to make your acquaintance.

TREVES. John. Your hand. She wishes to shake your hand.

MERRICK. Thank you for coming.

MRS. KENDAL. But it was my pleasure. Thank you. (*Exits, accompanied by* TREVES.)

TREVES. What a wonderful success. Do you know he's never shook a woman's hand before?

As lights fade MERRICK *sobs soundlessly, uncontrollably.*

SCENE 11

HE DOES IT WITH JUST
ONE HAND

Music. MERRICK *working on model of St. Phillip's church. Enter* DUCHESS. *At side* TREVES *ticks off a gift list.*

MERRICK. Your grace.

DUCHESS. How nicely the model is coming along, Mr. Merrick. I've come to say Happy Christmas, and that I hope you will enjoy this ring and remember your friend by it.

MERRICK. Your grace, thank you.

DUCHESS. I am very pleased to have made your acquaintance. (*Exits.*)

(*Enter* COUNTESS.)

COUNTESS. Please accept these silver-backed brushes and comb for Christmas, Mr. Merrick.

MERRICK. With many thanks, Countess.

COUNTESS. I am very pleased to have made your acquaintance. (*Exits.*)

(*Enter* LORD JOHN.)

LORD JOHN. Here's the silver-topped walking stick, Merrick. Make you a regular Piccadilly exquisite. Keep up the good work. Self-help is the best help. Example to us all.

MERRICK. Thank you, Lord John.

LORD JOHN. Very pleased to have made your acquaintance. (*Exits.*)

(*Enter* TREVES *and* PRINCESS ALEXANDRA.)

TREVES. Her Royal Highness Princess Alexandra.

PRINCESS. The happiest of Christmases, Mr. Merrick.

TREVES. Her Royal Highness has brought you a signed photograph of herself.

MERRICK. I am honored, your Royal Highness. It is the treasure of my possessions. I have written to His Royal Highness the Prince of Wales to thank him for the pheasants and woodcock he sent.

PRINCESS You are a credit to Mr. Treves, Mr. Merrick. Mr. Treves, you are a credit to medicine, to England, and to Christendom. I am so very pleased to have made your acquaintance.

(PRINCESS, TREVES *exit. Enter* MRS. KENDAL.)

MRS. KENDAL. Good news, John, Bertie says we may use the Royal Box whenever I like. Mrs. Keppel says it gives a unique perspective. And for Christmas, ivory-handled razors and toothbrush.

(*Enter* TREVES.)

TREVES. And a cigarette case, my boy, full of cigarettes!

MERRICK. Thank you. Very much.

MRS. KENDAL. Look Freddie, look. The model of St. Phillip's.

TREVES. It is remarkable, I know.

MERRICK. And I do it with just one hand, they all say.

MRS. KENDAL. You are an artist, John Merrick, an artist.

MERRICK. I did not begin to build at first. Not till I saw what St. Phillip's really was. It is not stone and steel and glass; it is an imitation of grace flying up and up from the mud. So I make my imitation of an imitation. But even in that is heaven to me, Mrs. Kendal.

TREVES. That thought's got a good line, John. Plato believed this was all a world of illusion and that artists made illusions of illusions of heaven.

MERRICK. You mean we are all just copies? Of originals?

TREVES. That's it.

MERRICK. Who made the copies?

TREVES. God. The Demi-urge.

MERRICK. (*Goes back to work.*) He should have used both hands shouldn't he?

Music. Puts another piece on St. Phillip's. Fadeout.

SCENE 12

WHO DOES HE REMIND
YOU OF?

TREVES, MRS. KENDAL.

TREVES. Why all those toilet articles, tell me? He is much too deformed to use any of them.

MRS. KENDAL. Props of course. To make himself. As I make me.

TREVES. You? You think of yourself.

MRS. KENDAL. Well. He is gentle, almost feminine. Cheerful, honest within limits, a serious artist in his way. He is almost like me.

(*Enter* BISHOP HOW.)

BISHOP. He is religious and devout. He knows salvation must radiate to us or all is lost, which it's certainly not.

(*Enter* GOMM.)

GOMM. He seems practical, like me. He has seen enough of daily evil to be thankful for small goods that come his way. He knows what side his bread is buttered on, and counts his blessings for it. Like me.

(*Enter* DUCHESS.)

DUCHESS. I can speak with him of anything. For I know he is discreet. Like me.

(*All exit except* TREVES.)

TREVES. How odd. I think him curious, compassionate, concerned about the world, well, rather like myself, Freddie Treves, 1889 AD.

(*Enter* MRS. KENDAL.)

MRS. KENDAL. Of course he is rather odd. And hurt. And helpless not to show the struggling. And so am I.

(*Enter* GOMM.)

GOMM. He knows I use him to raise money for the London, I am certain. He understands I would be derelict if I didn't. He is wary of any promise, yet he fits in well. Like me.

(*Enter* BISHOP HOW.)

BISHOP. I as a seminarist had many of the same doubts. Struggled as he does. And hope they may be overcome.

(*Enter* PRINCESS ALEXANDRA.)

PRINCESS. When my husband His Royal Highness Edward Prince of Wales asked Dr. Treves to be his personal surgeon, he said, "Dear Freddie, if you can put up with the Elephant bloke, you can surely put up with me."

(*All exit, except* TREVES. *Enter* LORD JOHN.)

LORD JOHN. See him out of fashion, Freddie. As he sees me. Social contacts critical. Oh—by the way—ignore the bloody papers; all lies. (*Exits.*)

TREVES. Merrick visibly worse than 86-87. That, as he rises higher in the consolations of society, he gets visibly more grotesque is proof definitive he is like me. Like his condition, which I make no sense of, I make no sense of mine.

Spot on MERRICK *placing another piece on St. Phillip's. Fadeout.*

SCENE 13

ANXIETIES OF THE SWAMP

MERRICK, *in spot, strains to listen:* TREVES, LORD JOHN *outside.*

TREVES. But the papers are saying you broke the contracts. They are saying you've lost the money.

LORD JOHN. Freddie, if I were such a scoundrel, how would I dare face investors like yourself. Broken contracts! I never considered them actual contracts— just preliminary things, get the old deal under way. An actual contract's something between gentlemen; and this attack on me shows they are no gentlemen. Now I'm only here to say the company remains a terribly attractive proposition. Don't you think? To recapitalize—if you could spare another—ah. (*Enter* GOMM.) Mr. Gomm. How good to see you. Just remarking how splendidly Merrick thrives here, thanks to you and Freddie.

GOMM. Lord John. Allow me: I must take Frederick from you. Keep him at work. It's in his contract. Wouldn't want him breaking it. Sort of thing makes the world fly apart, isn't it?

LORD JOHN. Yes. Well. Of course, mmm.

GOMM. Sorry to hear you're so pressed. Expect we'll see less of you around the London now?

LORD JOHN. Of course, I, actually—ah! Overdue actually. Appointment in the City. Freddie. Mr. Gomm. (*Exits.*)

TREVES. He plain fooled me. He was kind to Merrick.

GOMM. You have risen fast and easily, my boy. You've forgot how to protect yourself. Break now.

TREVES. It does not seem right somehow.

GOMM. The man's a moral swamp. Is that not clear yet? Is he attractive? Deceit often is. Friendly? Swindlers can be. Another loan? Not another cent. It may be your money, Freddie; but I will not tolerate laboring like a navvy that the London should represent honest charitable and compassionate science, and have titled swindlers mucking up the pitch. He has succeeded in destroying himself so rabidly, you ought not doubt an instant it was his real aim all along. He broke the contracts, gambled the money away, lied, and like an infant in his mess, gurgles and wants to do it again. Never mind details, don't want to know. Break and be glad. Don't hesitate. Today. One-man moral swamp. Don't be sucked in.

(*Enter* MRS. KENDAL.)

MRS. KENDAL. Have you seen the papers?

TREVES. Yes.

GOMM. Yes, yes. A great pity. Freddie: today. (*Exits.*)

MRS. KENDAL. Freddie?

TREVES. He has used us. I shall be all right. Come. (MRS. KENDAL, TREVES *enter to* MERRICK.) John: I shall not be able to stay this visit. I must, well, un-ravel a few things. Nurse Ireland and Snork are—?

MERRICK. Friendly and repectful Frederick.

TREVES. I'll look in in a few days.

MERRICK. Did I do something wrong?

MRS. KENDAL. No.

TREVES. This is a hospital. Not a marketplace. Don't forget it, ever. Sorry. Not you. Me. (*Exits.*)

MRS. KENDAL. Well. Shall we weave today? Don't you think weaving might be fun? So many things are fun. Most men really can't enjoy them. Their loss, isn't it? I like little activities which engage me; there's something ancient in it. I don't know. Before all this. Would you like to try? John?

MERRICK. Frederick said I may stay here for life.

MRS. KENDAL. And so you shall.

MERRICK. If he is in trouble?

MRS. KENDAL. Frederick is your protector, John.

MERRICK. If he is in trouble? (*He picks up small photograph.*)

MRS. KENDAL. Who is that? Ah, is it not your mother? She is pretty, isn't she?

MERRICK. Will Frederick keep his word with me, his contract, Mrs. Kendal? If he is in trouble.

MRS. KENDAL. What? Contract? Did you say?

MERRICK. And will you?

MRS. KENDAL. I? What? Will I?

MERRICK *silent. Puts another piece on model. Fadeout.*

SCENE 14

ART IS PERMITTED BUT NATURE FORBIDDEN

Rain. MERRICK *working.* MRS. KENDAL.

MERRICK. The Prince has a mistress. (*Silence.*) The Irishman had one. Everyone seems to. Or a wife. Some have both. I have concluded I need a mistress. It is bad enough not to sleep like others.

MRS. KENDAL. Sitting up, you mean. Couldn't be very restful.

MERRICK. I have to. Too heavy to lay down. My head. But to sleep alone; that is worst of all.

MRS. KENDAL. The artist expresses his love through his works. That is civilization.

MERRICK. Are you very shocked?

MRS. KENDAL. Why should I be?

MERRICK. Others would be.

MRS. KENDAL. I am not others.

MERRICK. I suppose it is hopeless.

MRS. KENDAL. Nothing is hopeless. However it is unlikely.

MERRICK. I thought you might have a few ideas.

MRS. KENDAL. I can guess who has ideas here.

MERRICK. You don't know something. I have never even seen a naked woman.

MRS. KENDAL. Surely in all the fairs you worked.

MERRICK. I mean a real woman.

MRS. KENDAL. Is one more real than another?

MERRICK. I mean like the ones in the theater. The opera.

MRS. KENDAL. Surely you can't mean they are more real.

MERRICK. In the audience. A woman not worn out early. Not deformed by awful life. A lady. Someone kept up. Respectful of herself. You don't know what fairgrounds are like, Mrs. Kendal.

MRS. KENDAL. You mean someone like Princess Alexandra?

MERRICK. Not so old.

MRS. KENDAL. Ah. Like Dorothy.

MERRICK. She does not look happy. No.

MRS. KENDAL. Lady Ellen?

MERRICK. Too thin.

MRS. KENDAL. Then who?

MERRICK. Certain women. They have a kind of ripeness. They seem to stop at a perfect point.

MRS. KENDAL. My dear she doesn't exist.

MERRICK. That is probably why I never saw her.

MRS. KENDAL. What would your friend Bishop How say of all this I wonder?

MERRICK. He says I should put these things out of my mind.

MRS. KENDAL. It that the best he can suggest?

MERRICK. I put them out of my mind. They reappeared, snap.

MRS. KENDAL. What about Frederick?

MERRICK. He would be appalled if I told him.

MRS. KENDAL. I am flattered. Too little trust has maimed my life. But that is another story.

MERRICK. What a rain. Are we going to read this afternoon?

MRS. KENDAL. Yes. Some women are lucky to look well, that is all. It is a rather arbitrary gift; it has no really good use, though it has uses, I will say that. Anyway it does not signify very much.

MERRICK. To me it does.

MRS. KENDAL. Well. You are mistaken.

MERRICK. What are we going to read?

MRS. KENDAL. Trust is very important you know. I trust you.

MERRICK. Thank you very much. I have a book of Thomas Hardy's here. He is a friend of Frederick's. Shall we read that?

MRS. KENDAL. Turn around a moment. Don't look.

MERRICK. Is this a game?

MRS. KENDAL. I would not call it a game. A surprise. (*She begins undressing.*)

MERRICK. What kind of a surprise?

MRS. KENDAL. I saw photographs of you. Before I met you. You didn't know that, did you?

MERRICK. The ones from the first time, in '84? No, I didn't.

MRS. KENDAL. I felt it was—unjust. I don't know why. I cannot say my sense of justice is my most highly developed characteristic. You may turn around again. Well. A little funny, isn't it?

MERRICK. It is the most beautiful sight I have seen. Ever.

MRS. KENDAL. If you tell anyone, I shall not see you again, we shall not read, we shall not talk, we shall do nothing. Wait. (*Undoes her hair.*) There. No illusions. Now. Well? What is there to say? "I am extremely pleased to have made your acquaintance?"

(*Enter* TREVES.)

TREVES. For God's sakes. What is going on here? What is going on?

MRS. KENDAL. For a moment, Paradise, Freddie. (*She begins dressing.*)

TREVES. But have you no sense of decency? Woman, dress yourself quickly. (*Silence.* MERRICK *goes to put another piece on St. Phillip's.*) Are you not ashamed? Do you know what you are? Don't you know what is forbidden?

Fadeout.

Scene 15

INGRATITUDE

Ross *in* Merrick's *room*.

Ross. I come actually to ask your forgiveness.

Merrick. I found a good home, Ross. I forgave you.

Ross. I was hoping we could work out a deal. Something new maybe.

Merrick. No.

Ross. See, I was counting on it. That you were kind-hearted. Like myself. Some things don't change. Got to put your money on the things that don't, I figure. I figure from what I read about you, you don't change. Dukes, Ladies coming to see you. Ask myself why? Figure it's same as always was. Makes 'em feel good about themselves by comparison. Them things don't change. There but for the grace of. So I figure you're selling the same service as always. To better clientele. Difference now is you ain't charging for it.

Merrick. You make me sound like a whore.

Ross. You are. I am. They are. Most are. No disgrace, John. Disgrace is to be a stupid whore. Give it for free. Not capitalize on the interest in you. Not to have a manager then is stupid.

Merrick. You see this church. I am building it. The people who visit are friends. Not clients. I am not a dog walking on its hind legs.

Ross. I was thinking. Charge these people. Pleasure of the Elephant Man's company. Something. Right spirit is everything. Do it in the right spirit, they'd pay happily. I'd take ten percent. I'd be okay with ten percent.

Merrick. Bad luck's made you daft.

Ross. I helped you, John. Discovered you. Was that daft? No. Only daftness was being at a goldmine without a shovel. Without proper connections. Like Treves has. What's daft? Ross sows, Treves harvests? It's not fair, is it John? When you think about it. I do think about it. Because I'm old. Got something in my throat. You may have noticed. Something in my lung here too. Something in my belly I guess too. I'm not a heap of health, am I? But I'd do well with ten percent. I don't need more than ten percent. Ten percent'd give me a future slightly better'n a cobblestone. This lot would pay, if you charged in the right spirit. I don't ask much.

MERRICK. They're the cream, Ross. They know it. Man like you tries to make them pay, they'll walk away.

Ross. I'm talking about doing it in the right spirit.

MERRICK. They are my friends. I'd lose everything. For you. Ross, you lived your life. You robbed me of forty-eight pounds nine shillings, tuppence. You left me to die. Be satisfied Ross. You've had enough. You kept me like an animal in darkness. You come back and want to rob me again. Will you not be satisfied? Now I am a man like others, you want me to return?

Ross. Had a woman yet?

MERRICK. Is that what makes a man?

Ross. In my time it'd do for a start.

MERRICK. Not what makes this one. Yet I am like others.

Ross. Then I'm condemned. I got no energy to try nothing new. I may well go to the dosshouse straight. Die there anyway. Between filthy dosshouse rags. Nothing in the belly but acid. I don't like pain, John. The future gives pain sense. Without a future— (*Pauses.*) Five percent? John?

MERRICK. I'm sorry, Ross. It's just the way things are.

ROSS. By god. Then I am lost.

Fadeout.

SCENE 16

NO RELIABLE GENERAL
ANESTHETIC HAS APPEARED
YET

TREVES, *reading, makes notes.* MERRICK *works.*

MERRICK. Frederick—do you believe in heaven? Hell? What about Christ? What about God? I believe in heaven. The Bible promises in heaven the crooked shall be made straight.

TREVES. So did the rack, my boy. So do we all.

MERRICK. You don't believe?

TREVES. I will settle for a reliable general anesthetic at this point. Actually, though—I had a patient once. A woman. Operated on her for—a woman's thing. Used ether to anesthetize. Tricky stuff. Didn't come out of it. Pulse stopped, no vital signs, absolutely moribund. Just a big white dead mackerel. Five minutes later, she fretted back to existence, like a lost explorer with a great scoop of the undiscovered.

MERRICK. She saw heaven?

TREVES. Well. I quote her: it was neither heavenly nor hellish. Rather like perambulating in a London fog. People drifted by, but no one spoke. London, mind you. Hell's probably the provinces. She was shocked it wasn't more exotic. But allowed as how had she stayed, and got used to the familiar, so to speak, it did have hints of becoming a kind of bliss. She fled.

MERRICK. If you do not believe—why did you send Mrs. Kendal away?

TREVES. Don't forget. It saved you once. My interference. You know well enough—it was not proper.

MERRICK. How can you tell? If you do not believe?

TREVES. There are still standards we abide by.

MERRICK. They make us happy because they are for our own good.

TREVES. Well. Not always.

MERRICK. Oh.

TREVES. Look, if you are angry, just say so.

MERRICK. Whose standards are they?

TREVES. I am not in the mood for this chipping away at the edges, John.

MERRICK. That do not always make us happy because they are not always for our own good?

TREVES. Everyone's. Well. Mine. Everyone's.

MERRICK. That woman's, that Juliet?

TREVES. Juliet?

MERRICK. Who died, then came back.

TREVES. Oh. I see. Yes. Her standards too.

MERRICK. So.

TREVES. So what?

MERRICK. Did you see her? Naked?

TREVES. When I was operating. Of course—

MERRICK. Oh.

TREVES. Oh what?

MERRICK. Is it okay to see them naked if you cut them up afterwards?

TREVES. Good Lord. I'm a surgeon. That is science.

MERRICK. She died. Mrs. Kendal didn't.

TREVES. Well, she came back too.

MERRICK. And Mrs. Kendal didn't. If you mean that.

TREVES. I am trying to read about anesthetics. There is simply no comparison.

MERRICK. Oh.

TREVES. Science is a different thing. This woman came to me to be. I mean, it is not, well, love, you know.

MERRICK. Is that why you're looking for an anesthetic.

TREVES. It would be a boon to surgery.

MERRICK. Because you don't love them.

TREVES. Love's got nothing to do with surgery.

MERRICK. Do you lose many patients?

TREVES. I—some.

MERRICK. Oh.

TREVES. Oh what? What does it matter? Don't you see? If I love, if any surgeon loves her or any patient or not, what does it matter? And what conceivable difference to you?

MERRICK. Because it is your standards we abide by.

TREVES. For God's sakes. If you are angry just say it. I won't turn you out. Say it: I am angry. Go on. I am angry. I am angry! I am angry!

MERRICK. I believe in heaven.

TREVES. And it is not okay. If they undress if you cut them up. As you put it. Make me sound like Jack the, Jack the Ripper.

MERRICK. No. You worry about anesthetics.

TREVES. Are you having me on?

MERRICK. You are merciful. I myself am proof. Is it not so? (*Pauses.*) Well? Is it not so?

TREVES. Well I. About Mrs. Kendal—perhaps I was wrong. I, these days that is, I seem to. Lose my head. Taking too much on perhaps. I do not know—what is in me these days.

MERRICK. Will she come back? Mrs. Kendal?

TREVES. I will talk to her again.

MERRICK. But—will she?

TREVES. No. I don't think so.

MERRICK. Oh.

TREVES. There are other things involved. Very. That is. Other things.

MERRICK. Well. Other things. I want to walk now. Think. Other things. (*Begins to exit. Pauses.*) Why? Why won't she? (*Silence.* MERRICK *exits.*)

TREVES. Because I don't want her here when you die. (*He slumps in chair.*)

Fadeout.

SCENE 17

CRUELTY IS AS NOTHING TO
KINDNESS

TREVES *asleep in chair dreams the following:* MERRICK *and* GOMM *dressed as* Ross *in foreground.*

MERRICK. If he is merely papier maché and paint, a swindler and a fake—

GOMM. No, no, a genuine Dorset dreamer in a moral swamp. Look—he has so forgot how to protect himself he's gone to sleep.

MERRICK. I must examine him. I would not keep him for long, Mr. Gomm.

GOMM. It would be an inconvenience, Mr. Merrick. He is a mainstay of our institution.

MERRICK. Exactly that brought him to my attention. I am Merrick. Here is my card. I am with the mutations cross the road.

GOMM. Frederick, stand up. You must understand. He is very very valuable. We have invested a great deal in him. He is personal surgeon to the Prince of Wales.

MERRICK. But I only wish to examine him. I had not of course dreamed of changing him.

GOMM. But he is a gentleman and a good man.

MERRICK. Therefore exemplary for study as a cruel or deviant one would not be.

GOMM. Oh very well. Have him back for breakfast time or you feed him. Frederick, stand up. Up you bloody donkey, up!

TREVES, *still asleep, stands up. Fadeout.*

SCENE 18

WE ARE DEALING WITH AN EPIDEMIC

TREVES *asleep.* MERRICK *at lecturn.*

MERRICK. The most striking feature about him, note, is the terrifying normal head. This allowed him to lie down normally, and therefore to dream in the exclusive personal manner, without the weight of others' dreams accumulating to break his neck. From the brow projected a normal vision of benevolent enlightenment, what we believe to be a kind of self-mesmerized state. The mouth, deformed by satisfaction at being at the hub of the best of existent worlds, was rendered therefore utterly incapable of self-critical speech, thus of the ability to change. The heart showed signs of worry at this unchanging yet untenable state. The back was horribly stiff from being kept against a wall to face the discontent of a world ordered for his convenience. The surgeon's hands were well-developed and strong, capable of the most delicate carvings-up, for others' own good. Due also to the normal head, the right arm was of enormous power; but, so incapable of the distinction between the assertion of authority and the charitable act of giving, that it was often to be found disgustingly beating others—for their own good. The left arm was slighter and fairer, and may be seen in typical position, hand covering the genitals which were treated as a sullen colony in constant need of restriction, governance, punishment. For their own good. To add a further burden to his trouble the wretched man when a boy developed a disabling spiritual duality, therefore was unable to feel what others feel, nor reach harmony with them. Please. (TREVES *shrugs*.) He would thus be denied all means of escape from those he had tormented.

(PINS *enter*.)

FIRST PIN. Mr. Merrick. You have shown a profound and unknown disorder to us. You have said when he leaves here, it is for his prior life again. I do not think it ought to be permitted. It is a disgrace. It is a pity and a disgrace. It is an indecency in fact. It may be a danger in ways we do not know. Something ought to be done about it.

MERRICK. We hope in twenty years we will understand enough to put an end to this affliction.

FIRST. PIN. Twenty years! Sir, that is unacceptable!

MERRICK. Had we caught it early, it might have been different. But his condition has already spread

both East and West. The truth is, I am afraid, we are
dealing with an epidemic.

MERRICK *puts another piece on St. Phillip's.* PINS *exit.*
    TREVES *starts awake. Fadeout.*

SCENE 19

THEY CANNOT MAKE OUT
WHAT HE IS SAYING

MERRICK, BISHOP How *in background.* BISHOP *ges-
    tures,* MERRICK *on knees.* TREVES *foreground.*
    Enter* GOMM.

GOMM. Still beavering away for Christ?
TREVES. Yes.
GOMM. I got your report. He doesn't know, does he?
TREVES. The Bishop?
GOMM. I meant Merrick.
TREVES. No.
GOMM. I shall be sorry when he dies.
TREVES. It will not be unexpected anyway.
GOMM. He's brought the hospital quite a lot of good
repute. Quite a lot of contributions too, for that mat-
ter. In fact, I like him; never regretted letting him
stay on. Though I didn't imagine he'd last this long.
TREVES. His heart won't sustain him much longer.
It may even give out when he gets off his bloody
knees with that bloody man.
GOMM. What is it, Freddie? What has gone sour for
you?
TREVES. It is just—it is the overarc of things, quite
inescapable that he's achieved greater and greater

normality, his condition's edged him closer to the grave. So—a parable of growing up? To become more normal is to die? More accepted to worsen? He—it is just a mockery of everything we live by.

GOMM. Sorry Freddie. Didn't catch that one.

TREVES. Nothing has gone sour. I do not know.

GOMM. Cheer up, man. You are knighted. Your clients will be kings. Nothing succeeds my boy like success. (*Exits.*)

(BISHOP *comes from* MERRICK's *room.*)

BISHOP. I find my sessions with him utterly moving, Mr. Treves. He struggles so. I suggested he might like to be confirmed; he leaped at it like a man lost in a desert to an oasis.

TREVES. He is very excited to do what others do if he thinks it is what others do.

BISHOP. Do you cast doubt, sir, on his faith?

TREVES. No, sir, I do not. Yet he makes all of us think he is deeply like ourselves. And yet we're not like each other. I conclude that we have polished him like a mirror, and shout hallelujah when he reflects us to the inch. I have grown sorry for it.

BISHOP. I cannot make out what you're saying. Is something troubling you, Mr. Treves?

TREVES. Corsets. How about corsets? Here is a pamphlet I've written due mostly to the grotesque ailments I've seen caused by corsets. Fashion overrules me, of course. My patients do not unstrap themselves of corsets. Some cannot—you know, I have so little time in the week, I spend Sundays in the poor-wards; to keep up with work. Work being twenty-year-old women who look an abused fifty with worn-outed-ness; young men with appalling industrial conditions

I turn out as soon as possible to return to their labors. Happily most of my patients are not poor. They are middle class. They overeat and drink so grossly, they destroy nature in themselves and all around them so fervidly, they will not last. Higher up, sir, above this middle class, I confront these same—deformities— bulged out by unlimited resources and the ruthlessness of privilege into the most scandalous dissipation yoked to the grossest ignorance and constraint. I counsel against it where I can. I am ignored of course. Then, what, sir, could be troubling me? I am an extremely successful Englishman in a successful and respected England which informs me daily by the way it lives that it wants to die. I am in despair in fact. Science, observation, practice, deduction, having led me to these conclusions, can no longer serve as consolation. I apparently see things others don't.

BISHOP. I do wish I understand you better, sir. But as for consolation, there is in Christ's church consolation.

TREVES. I am sure we were not born for mere consolation.

BISHOP. But look at Mr. Merrick's happy example.

TREVES. Oh yes. You'd like my garden too. My dog, my wife, my daughter, pruned, cropped, pollarded and somewhat stupefied. Very happy examples, all of them. Well. Is it all we know how to finally do with— whatever? Nature? Is it? Rob it? No, not really, not nature I mean. Ourselves really. Myself really. Robbed, that is. You do see of course, can't figure out, really, what else to do with them. Can we? (*Laughs.*)

BISHOP. It is not exactly clear, sir.

TREVES. I am an awfully good gardener. Is that clear? By god I take such good care of anything, any- thing you, we, are convinced—are you not convinced,

him I mean, is not very dangerously human? I mean
how could he be? After what we've given him? What
you like, sir, is that he is so grateful for patrons, so
greedy to be patronized, and no demands, no rights,
no hopes; past perverted, present false, future nil.
What better could you ask? He puts up with all of it.
Of course I do mean taken when I say given, as in
what, what, what we have given him, but. You knew
that. I'll bet. Because. I. I. I. I—

BISHOP. Do you mean Charity? I cannot tell what
you are saying.

TREVES. Help me. (*Weeps.*)

(BISHOP *consoles him.*)

MERRICK. (*Rises, puts last piece on St. Phillip's.*) It
is done.

Fadeout.

SCENE 20

THE WEIGHT OF DREAMS

MERRICK *alone, looking at model. Enter* SNORK *with
lunch.*

SNORK. Lunch, Mr. Merrick. I'll set it up. Maybe
you'd like a walk after lunch. April's doing wonders
for the gardens. (*A funeral procession passes slowly
by.*) My mate Will, his sister died yesterday. Twenty-
eight she was. Imagine that. Wife was sick, his sister
nursed her. Was a real bloom that girl. Now wife
okay, sister just ups and dies. It's all so—what's

that word? Forgot it. It means chance-y. Well. Forgot it. Chance-y'll do. Have a good lunch. (*Exits.*)

(MERRICK *eats a little, breathes on model, polishes it, goes to bed, arms on knees, head on arms, the position in which he must sleep.*)

MERRICK. Chancey? (*Sleeps.*)

(*Enter* PINHEADS *singing.*)

PINS.
We are the Queens of the Cosmos
Beautiful darkness' empire
Darkness darkness, light's true flower,
Here is eternity's finest hour
Sleep like others you learn to admire
Be like your mother, be like your sire.

(*They straighten* MERRICK *out to normal sleep position. His head tilts over too far. His arms fly up clawing the air. He dies. As light fades,* SNORK *enters.*)

SNORK. I remember it, Mr. Merrick. The word is "arbitrary." Arbitrary. It's all so—oh. Hey! Hey! The Elephant Man is dead!

Fadeout.

SCENE 21

FINAL REPORT TO THE
INVESTORS

GOMM *reading,* TREVES *listening.*

GOMM. "To the Editor of the *Times*. Sir; In November, 1886, you were kind enough to insert in the *Times* a letter from me drawing attention to the case of Joseph Merrick—"

TREVES. John. John Merrick.

GOMM. Well. "—known as the Elephant Man. It was one of singular and exceptional misfortune" et cetera et cetera ". . . debarred from earning his livelihood in any other way than being exhibited to the gaze of the curious. This having been rightly interfered with by the police . . ." et cetera et cetera, "with great difficulty he succeeded somehow or other in getting to the door of the London Hospital where through the kindness of one of our surgeons he was sheltered for a time." And then . . . and then . . . and . . . ah. "While deterred by common humanity frc 〉 evicting him again into the open street, I wrote to ᵧou and from that moment all difficulty vanished; the sympathy of many was aroused, and although no other fitting refuge was offered, a sufficient sum was placed at my disposal, apart from the funds of the hospital, to maintain him for what did not promise to be a prolonged life. As "

TREVES, I forgot. The coroner said it was death by asphyxiation. The weight of the head crushed the windpipe.

GOMM. Well. I go on to say about how he spent his time here, that all attempted to alleviate his misery, that he was visited by the highest in the land et cetera, et cetera, that in general he joined our lives as best he could, and: "In spite of all this indulgence, he was quiet and unassuming, grateful for all that was done for him, and conformed readily to the restrictions which were necessary." Will that do so far, do you think?

TREVES. Should think it would.

GOMM. Wouldn't add anything else, would you?

TREVES. Well. He was highly intelligent. He had an acute sensibility; and worst for him, a romantic imagination. No, no. Never mind. I am really not certain of any of it. (*Exits.*)

GOMM. "I have given these details thinking that those who sent money to use for his support would like to know how their charity was used. Last Friday afternoon, though apparently in his usual health, he quietly passed away in his sleep. I have left in my hands a small balance of the money for his support, and this I now propose after paying certain gratuities, to hand over to the general funds of the hospital. This course I believe will be consonant with the wishes of the contributors.

"It was the courtesy of the *Times* in inserting my letter in 1886 that procured for this afflicted man a comfortable protection during the last years of a previously wretched existence, and I desire to take this opportunity of thankfully acknowledging it.

"I am sir, your obedient servant,

F. C. Carr Gomm

"House Committee Room, London Hospital."

15 April 1890.

(TREVES *reenters.*)

TREVES. I did think of one small thing.

GOMM. It's too late, I'm afraid. It is done. (*Smiles.*)

Hold before fadeout.

THE ELEPHANT MAN
TRANSITIONS (*The Orderly*)

Mopping

On cue light.

1. Enter from u.l. with bucket from u.l. with bucket and mop.
2. Place bucket d.l. of bath tub and mop l. of tub and u. of table.

As WILL enters.

3. Begin talking to WILL and carry bucket, leaving it c., u. of L post #1 and R post #1.

WILL holds out mop.

4. Take the mop and leave it in the bucket after wetting own mop.
5. Begin mopping outside l. towards c.

After WILL has extinguished lights and takes his mop.

6. X back to bucket and move it u. and l.; continue mopping.

As TREVES arrives outside r.

7. Acknowledge TREVES, and continue mopping.

As GOMM enters.

8. Move the bucket to l. of tub and continue mopping u.s.

"On Wimpole Street."

9. Pick up the bucket and x u., exiting u.r.

Lecture

"Up, you bloody donkey, up!"

1. Enter from R#2, xing outside r. to d.r., pick up d.r. arm-chair. X back u., outside r. and set it below and r. of R post #3, exiting u.l.

Carnival

Carnival sounds.

1. Enter from L#2, dressed as a Carnie. X outside l. and place stip lights from stage floor to deck between L post #1 and L post #2. Exit off L#2.

"Doesn't hurt. Doesn't hurt."

1. Enter from L#2, still as Carnie, pull curtain u.s. to L post #2 and tie it.
2. X d. outside and replace strip lights to stage floor. Exit L#2.

Liverpool
"Robbed."

1. Enter from L#, x below L post #2, life the trunk and place it d.l., inside L post #1.
2. X to chair below L post #1, and set it u. of post.
3. X outside l. to u.l. and x to r. of c.

GOMM x's u.s. and hands card.

1. Exit u.r. with card.

Sandwich
1. "Help me" light fade.

1. Enter from R#2 with bench and x outside r. and place it d. of R post #1, perpendicular to the audience.
2. X u.c. to d.s. of tub and move it down to the first spike marks.
3. X to d.l., pick up trunk with cape and cap-mask and carry it r. to outside r. and off R#2.

First Bishop
"This is not helping him."

1. Enter from L#2, x to above the table and move it to extreme d.s. position.
2. X to chair u. of L post #1 and xing outside l., place it in d.s. position.

As TREVES is changing into lab coat.

3. X outside l., above TREVES and L post #1 and pick up lunch tray on u.s. end of table. X l. of tub and signal WILL off l. and exit L#2.

Firing Scene
"Is there something wrong, Mr.
 Gomm. With us."

1. Enter from L#2, xing below
 L post #2 to u. of table and
 move chair to r. of L post
 #1, facing off r.
2. Move table to extreme u.s.
 position.
3. X u.s., to above WILL and to
 his r.

WILL sends off.

4. Exit u.r.

First Kendal
"Boom . . . boom . . . boom."

1. Enter from L#2 with silver
 tray with decanter and two
 glasses and set it on the u.r.
 corner of table with the bottle
 to the r.
2. Push the table to the extreme
 d.s. position.
3. X l. of table, pick up the
 armchair and move it outside
 l. to d.s. position.

MRS. KENDAL x's u.s.

4. X back around L post #1 to
 above the tub and pull it to
 its extreme u.s. position.
5. X l. of tub and below it to
 outside r., below R post #2.
 Pull the curtain d.s. from R
 post #3 to R post #2.
6. X above R post #3, l. of tub
 to below it.

MERRICK arrives u.s.

7. Finish tying the ties on
 MERRICK's hospital gown.

MERRICK x's to bed.

8. X to l. of tub, roll up shirt
 sleeves and begin scrubbing
 the tub with rag at drain.

TREVES rises and x's d.l.

1. Rise and x above the tub to
 the r. of it and continue to
 scrub the tub from that side.

"Famous for it."

1. Finish tub and exit u.r. above
 the bed.

Second Kendal
"He must be lonely indeed."

1. Enter from L#2, xing outside l. to l. of desk, open the drawer and remove sketch pad and pencil and open it c. of table.
2. Pick up armchair and place it u. of L post #1.
3. X to above table and move it one foot above spike marks, the d.s. end of table even with L post #1.
4. Pick up tray with decanter and glasses and exit L#2.

END OF ACT I

Like Me
". . . both hands, shouldn't he?"

1. Enter from L#2 with d.l. wing piece and leave it u.s. of model on the table. Exit L#2.

Anxieties
"I can make no sense of mine."

1. Enter from R#2 with two "Financial Times," x outside r. to Treves and hand one to him.
2. X outside r. to u.r. opening the paper. X to chair r. of L post #3 and sit, reading.

Gomm motions to stand.

1. Rise, put paper on chair and x to u. of bed.

"Come."

1. Release the bed and move it to its d.s. position.
2. X back to u.l. to chair with paper on it, pick it up and exit u.l.

Ross II
Kendal look with cape.

1. Enter from L#2 with d.r. wing piece and Thomas Hardy book.
2. Hand wing piece immediately to Merrick across the table.
3. X d.s. below the table and leave book on d.s. end of table.

4. Pull the table to its extreme d.s. position.
5. X back l. of table and place the armchair u. of L post #1.
6. X u., above the gift chair, and stand to its r. for the scene.

Picnic
"I am lost."

1. X to l. of bed, pausing momentarily for MERRICK to clear.
2. X above bench to r. of table and pick up the model, x to u.l. and place it.
3. X to below the gift table, lay down the gold-framed picture and lift the entire table, xing u.s. and off u.r.

Anesthetic
MERRICK-TREVES *look*.

1. Enter from u.l. with long and short towers. Place long tower on d.r. corner and the short tower on d.l. corner of the model.
2. Lift the model with the towers and place it d.s. of bench, l. of it.
3. Pick up long tower, x below the bench and set it c. of bed from below it.
4. X back l. to the table and strike the picnic basket and umbrella and x outside l. to L#2.

Dream
". . . her here, when you die."

1. Enter from L#2, xing below L post #2, to d.c. Pick up bench and set it d. of R post #1, angling it u.
2. X back to u. and l. to L post #2 and when TREVES sits asleep in chair and MERRICK's coat is almost on, pulll curtain across to R post #2.

3. Stand below and l. of R post #2 for the scene.

Corset
MERRICK *turns to* TREVES.

1. Pull curtain back across to L post #2.
2. X d. to chair u. of L post #1 and move it to its d.s. position. Exit outside l. off L#2.

Death
"It is done."

1. Enter L#2, x outside l. to below L post #1. Lift the armchair to u.s. end of table, facing off l.
2. X above the table and move it to its u.s. position. Exit L#2.

Final Report
"The Elephant Man is . . ."

1. In blackout, enter from R#2, x to above bed and pull it to its u.s. position. Exit u.r.

". . . to use for his support."

1. Enter from u.l., x to u.c. and x slowly d. to c., between L and R posts #2 and #3.

END OF PLAY

COSTUME PLOT

Inventory

TREVES, BELGIAN POLICEMAN

(Act One—TREVES)
  Lab coat with small pin in lapel
  Blue-grey flecked frock coat
  Blue-grey flecked waistcoat
  Blue-grey flecked trousers
  Suspenders
  White neckband shirt with winged collar
  Blue waistcoat
  Cuff links
  Black shoes
  Black socks
  Grey felt top hat
  Grey gloves
  Grey spats
  Watch and chain
  Collar studs
  Navy and red cravat with stick pin
  Taupe cravat with stick pin
  Spectacles
(Act Two—TREVES)
  Black cutaway coat
  Striped trousers
  Grey waistcoat
  Beige cravat
  Suspenders
  Red stick pin
  Dark grey frock coat
  Dark grey waistcoat
  Dark grey trousers
  Dark print cravat
  Suspenders
  Stick pin
(BELGIAN POLICEMAN)
  Navy uniform coat
  Black gaiters
  Navy Gendarme hat with white band
  White gloves

65

PINHEAD II, MRS. KENDAL

(PINHEAD II)
  Long johns with frill and red mittens attached
  Leopard skin
  Tu-tu
  Frilled petticoat as a cape
  Cone hat
  Ruff
  Baldric
  Tights
  Black boots
(Act One—MRS. KENDAL)
  Copper bodice with four jewelled pins
  Copper skirt
  Bustle
  Brown beaded and crocheted reticule
  Beige short kid gloves
  Beige socks
  Beige two-tone boots
  Copper net and feathered hat
  Earrings
(Act Two—MRS. KENDAL)
  Beige lace blouse
  Black satin and velvet embroidered skirt with gold chain
    attached
  Black fur and beaver jacket
  Black velvet hat
  Long white kid gloves
  Green rep and satin skirt
  Russian blouse
  Silk and lace camisole
  Red and ivory sash
  Gold leather belt
  Cream cashmire and paisley shawl

WHORE, PINHEAD I, SANDWICH, PRINCESS ALEXANDRA

(WHORE)
  Paisley jacket
  Grey skirt with black underskirt attached

Blue and lace dickie with jabot
Red hat with black tie ribbons
Fur muff
Beige short gloves
(PINHEAD I)
  Long johns with frill and mittens attached and gold embroidered cuff
  Tu-tu
  Ruff
  Frilled petticoat cape
  Leopard skin
  Baldric
  Cone hat
  Grey tights
  Black boots
(MISS SANDWICH)
  Navy and grey cape
  Taupe costume with ecru linen collar and cuffs—fob watch on breast
  White cotton petticoat
  Blue bib apron
  Blue and ecru cap
  Black bag
(PRINCESS ALEXANDRA)
  Blue satin and velvet costume
  Blue and black feathered hat
  Hyacinth shot taffeta underskirt
  Bustle
  Black kid gloves
  Black net dickie
  Earrings

PINHEAD MANAGER, LONDON POLICEMAN, WILL, LORD JOHN

(WILL)
  Brown porter's tunic
  Brown porter's pants
  Brown porter's hat
  Beige cravat
  White apron
  Black lacing boots

Brown bowler hat (Tuppence)

(PINHEAD MANAGER)
Red tail coat
White jodphurs
White shirt with 2 collars and 2 bowties, a black velvet
  waistcoat and brocade waistcoat all sewn together
Black belt
Leather studded belt
Black top hat
Black boots
White gauntlets
Steel rimmed glasses

(POLICEMAN)
Bobby tunic
Bobby trousers
Inverness style cape
Bobby helmet
White gloves

(LORD JOHN)
Black cutaway coat
Black and grey striped trousers
Ivory brocade waistcoat
Beige cravat
White dress shirt
Wing collar
Grey blue sash
Pocket watch and chain
Blue ribbon
Gold medallion
Two medals
Cufflinks
Suspenders
Black Wellingtons
Black socks
Black silk hat
Black hat drape
Black trousers
Black and white cravat
Grey spats
Grey gloves
Blue jewel
Back and front studs

ORDERLY, CARNIE, ASSISTANT CONDUCTOR

(ORDERLY)
Porter's tunic
Porter's hat
Porter's trousers
White apron
Beige cravat
White neckband shirt
White collar
Black Wellingtons
Black socks
Back and front studs
(CARNIE)
Maroon overcoat
Uniform peaked cap
Brown and cream plaid muffler
(ASSISTANT CONDUCTOR)
Black uniform tunic
Black peaked cap
Black string tie
Uniform waistcoat
Black wool gloves

GOMM, POLICEMAN, CONDUCTOR

(Act One—GOMM)
Grey frock coat
Grey waistcoat
Grey trousers
Suspenders
White neckband shirt
Wing collar
Dark print cravat
Coral pin
Black socks
Black shoes
Grey spats
Pince nez
Pocket watch and chain
Cufflinks
Back and front studs
White lab coat with badge in lapel

(ACT TWO—GOMM)
  Black cutaway coat
  Black striped trousers
  Suspenders
  Dove grey waistcoat
  Spotted cravat
  Green stud
  Watch chain
  Grey frock coat
  Grey waistcoat
  Grey trousers
  Rust cravat
  Suspenders
  Green stud
(POLICEMAN)
  Navy tunic
  Navy blue helmet
  Navy trousers
  Navy cape
  White gloves
(CONDUCTOR)
  Grey uniform coat with red trim
  Grey and red uniform hat
  Grey wool scarf

ROSS, BISHOP, SNORK

(Ross)
  Black and grey checked coat
  Wool shawl
  Navy wool cap
  Tweed trousers
  Suspenders
  Grey shirt
  Fringed fawn silk scarf
  Cord embroidered blue belt
  Brown suede belt with three purses
  Brown suede boots
  Grey wool mittens
  Red military belt
(BISHOP)
  Black cassock

Black checked trousers
Suspenders
White neckband shirt
Wing collar
Cream wool stock with linen embroidered tabs
Black gloves
Black Homburg
Ivory orale (stoll)
Black socks
Black shoes
Black spats
Cufflinks
Back and front studs
(SNORK)
Porter's uniform jacket
Porter's uniform cap
Porter's uniform trousers
Beige cravat
White apron
Black arm band

JOHN MERRICK

(Act One—JOHN MERRICK)
Coarse cotton loin cloth
Dirty white blanket cape
Black cap with grey mask
Hospital gown
(Act Two—JOHN MERRICK)
Light grey trousers
Blue-grey waistcoat
White neckband shirt
Wing collar
Grey silk stock and scarf
Grey cutaway coat
Black velvet slippers
Back and front studs
Cuff links
Stick pin

CELLIST

(CELLIST)
  Black cutaway coat
  Grey and black striped trousers
  Ivory brocade waistcoat
  Black and white cravat
  White neckband shirt
  Black socks
  Grey spats
  Black shoes
  Wing collar
  Back and front studs

COSTUME PRESET

Stage Right
(WILL)
  Bowler hat
(ROSS)
  Plaid coat
  Wool cap
  Two wool shawls
(SNORK)
  Porter's tunic
  Porter trousers
  White apron
  Cravat
  Cap
  Black armband
(BISHOP)
  Cassock
  Ecru collar
  Black gloves
  Black bowler hat
(BELGIUM POLICEMAN)
  Police overcoat
  Gaiters
  Cap with visor
  White gloves
(LONDON POLICEMAN)
  Tunic

Pants
Cape
Helmet
White gloves
(CONDUCTOR)
  Grey overcoat
  Grey muffler
  Grey uniform cap
  Grey gloves
(PINHEAD MANAGER)
  Boots
  Pants
  Waitcoat
  Red coat
  Belt
  Gloves
  Spectacles
(MISS SANDWICH)
  Taupe dress
  Petticoat
  Cape
  Cap
  Purse
(PINHEAD I)
  Tu-tu
  Cape
  Ruff
  Hat
  Sash
(GOMM)
  Lab coat (Pressed)
(TREVES)
  Lab coat (Pressed and set on stage by props)
(MERRICK)
  Hospital gown (Pressed and set on stage by props)
(BISHOP)
  Stole (Pressed)
(TREVES)
  Waistcoat
  Cravat
(SNORK)
  Apron

Stage Left
(London Policeman)
  Pants
  Tunic
  Cape
  Helmet
  White gloves
(Assistant Conductor)
  Jacket (Waistcoat and string tie underdressed)
  Pants
  Cap
  Black wool gloves
(Carnie)
  Dark maroon overcoat
  Brown plaid muffler
  Vizored cap
(Merrick)
  Grey cutaway coat
  Two stage hand orderly costumes
  Understudy London Policeman

Stage Right
(Pinhead, Sandwich)
  Pinhead baldric, tu tu, cape, ruff, hat from dressing room to
    s.r. quick change.
  These are placed in basket in the following sequence: Cape,
    tu-tu, baldric, hat and neck ruffle on black muff (side of
    table).
  Miss Sandwich white petticoat, taupe dress with apron
    attached, navy cape, nurses' cap and handbag from dress-
    ing room to s.r. quick change room.
(Bishop How, Snork, etc.)
  Drop cloth and chair placed behind s.r. quick change booth.
  How white shirt and black trousers on hangers placed on
    hangers placed on back wall.
  How black shoes with spats on placed near chair.
  How beige tie put on How robe.
  Snork apron put with Snork taupe suit.
(Lord John, Pinhead Manager, etc.)
  Pinhead Manager red coat, waistcoats, shirt, white pants,
    pants set on farthest chair.
(Gomm, Bobbie, Conductor, etc.)
  Bobbie jacket placed with pants on top.
  Bobbie helmet with white gloves on table.

(TREVES, BELGIAN POLICEMAN)
    BELGIAN POLICEMAN hat with white gloves and leggings
    placed on small table outside the change room.

Stage Left
(LORD JOHN, PINHEAD MANAGER, LONDON POLICEMAN, etc.)
    LONDON POLICEMAN pants, tunic, cape, helmet and white
    gloves set.
(MERRICK)
    Grey cutaway coat placed.
(ORDERLY, CONDUCTOR, CARNIE, etc.)
    ASSISTANT CONDUCTOR jacket, pants, cap, wool gloves with
    waistcoat and string tie under-dressed placed.
    CARNIE dark maroon overcoat, brown plaid muffler with
    visored hat placed.
    Two stage hand orderly costumes placed.

QUICK CHANGE DRESSER #1—S.R.

ACT I

1. Help Ross into shawl and plaid coat   S.R.
2. Set BOBBY, CONDUCTOR grey coat on chair.
   Place BOBBY cape and tunic and pants on top.   S.R.
3. Help WHORE out of her costume.
   Change to PINHEAD neck piece, sash, shirt, tutu-etc.
   Complete PINHEAD.
   Hang up WHORE costume.   S.R.
4. Remove BOBBY cape, take billie club.
   Help into CONDUCTOR grey coat.   S.R.
5. Move the BELGIAN POLICEMAN to center chair.
   Put on BELGIAN POLICEMAN overcoat.
   When he sits, put on the left and right giaters.   S.R.
6. Remove PINHEAD costume.
   Put on MISS SANDWICH white petticoat, taupe dress,
   cape, nurse's cap and hand black handbag.   S.R.
7. Remove CONDUCTOR costume.
   Put on GOMM spats and lab coat.   S.R.
8. Help into BISHOP How cassock and tie.
   Place hat and black gloves on table.
   Pick up from back of change room, Ross costume.
   Hang shirt belts, etc.   S.R.

9. Set out SNORK costume.
   Take MERRICK's shoes from R#1 to R#2.
   Set out apron with pocket up.
   Help SNORK into pants, hold tunic, slip apron over
   head and tie.   S.R.
10. Move Ross scarf and tweed pants to chair, where
    shoes were left.   S.R.
11. Take to dressing rooms:
    a. MERRICK blanket cape.
    b. Ross hanger with shirts and belts.
    c. GOMM grey frock coat.
    d. PINHEAD vest.
    e. Black vest.   S.R.

INTERMISSION

1. In dressing room, help PRINCESS ALEXANDRA into
   dress.
2. Take MRS. KENDAL's Russian blouse, sash and green
   skirt from dressing room to S.R. change booth.

ACT II

1. Help into BISHOP cassock.   S.R.
2. Help into Ross checked coat with grey scarf.   S.R.
3. Set up MRS. KENDAL change:
   a. Green skirt over head
   b. Russian blouse
   c. Sash
   d. Shawl   S.R.
4. Help Ross remove coat and scarf.   S.R.
5. Help MRS. KENDAL remove green skirt.
   Help into MRS. KENDAL camisole, black skirt, hat and
   jacket   S.R.
6. Help GOMM into Ross coat and hat.   S.R.
7. Help MRS. KENDAL into green skirt.   S.R.
   Hang Ross checked coat and cap.
   Hang MRS. KENDAL shawl.
   Help DRESSER #2.
   Take to Wardrobe room lab coat and vest to be
   pressed.
   Take dark grey coat to GOMM's dressing room.   S.R.

QUICK CHANGE DRESSER #2—S.L.
ACT I

1. Take WILL cap and apron and place on prop table
   temporarily to be taken to S.L. later.   S.R.
2. Take WILL costume (cravat, tunic, pants, boots) off
   and help into PINHEAD MANAGER—white britches,
   breakaway vest, red coat, belt, top hat, gauntlet,
   spectacles, riding boots. As soon as completed take
   complete WILL costume and BISHOP white stole
   to S.L.   S.R.
3. Help ORDERLY change into maroon coat.
   Set scarf in hat on the table.   S.L.
4. Help ORDERLY out of maroon coat and help change
   into ASSISTANT CONDUCTOR—black string tie, vest,
   jacket and cap.   S.L.
5. Gather together ORDERLY tunic, cravat, cap and
   apron and put to one side to be taken to S.R.
   later.   S.L.
6. Lay out WILL orderly tunic and pants on back of
   chair.
   Place shoes by the table.
   Place apron, cravat, cap, glasses case on table.
   Place LONDON POLICEMAN trousers on top and table
   and chair so that he can put these on first.   S.L.
7. Help change out of PINHEAD MANAGER red coat,
   breakaway vest.
   Pull LONDON POLICEMAN trousers over white jodphurs and high boots.
   Help into LONDON POLICEMAN tunic, cape, helmet,
   and gloves.   S.L.
8. Immediately take ORDERLY tunic, cravat, cap and
   apron to S.R. and lay out for quick change. Tunic
   placed on chair with hat in pocket. Apron and
   cravat placed on prop table ready to put on.
   Help ORDERLY out of ASSISTANT CONDUCTOR clothes.
   He will drop jacket, waistcoat, tie, cap and gloves
   on floor, and sit on chair. Pull off black pants.
   Help ORDERLY into apron, cravat, trousers.   S.R.
9. After entrance, gather ASSISTANT CONDUCTOR uniform and hang waist coat and string tie on wire
   hanger and leave on clothes line to be taken to
   dressing room.

Return jacket, pants, cap and gloves to S.L.   S.R.

10. LONDON POLICEMAN completing change to WILL,
    previously laid out. Assist to complete.   S.L.

11. Hang up ASSISTANT CONDUCTOR, CARNIE, LONDON
    POLICEMAN *and* PINHEAD MANAGER.
    Take PINHEAD MANAGER to S.R., leaving the boots
    for next trip across.   S.L.

12. Remove GOMM's lab coat as he exits, put it on a
    hanger and take to S.L.   S.R.

13. Hang GOMM's lab coat on rack and return to S.R.
    with PINHEAD MANAGER riding boots.   S.L.

14. Help SNORK out of his uniform.
    Hang jacket, apron cravat on hanger on clothes line
    and snap on mourning band.
    Place pants and elastic garters near pass door for
    later use.

15. End of act, take TREVES lab coat from him and
    hang on clothes line for property man to pre-set.
    (PROP MAN will bring off TREVES grey tweed coat
    and hang on clothes line.   S.R.

ACT II

1. During gift scene, take MERRICK hospital gown from
   dressing room to wardrobe and TREVES tweed coat
   to TREVES dressing room.   S.R.

2. Return immediately to assist BISHOP out of
   costume.
   Assist BISHOP into Ross costume with help of Quick
   Change dresser #1.   S.R.

3. As Ross enters, MRS. KENDAL will hand carpet bag.   S.R.

4. GOMM exits. Take off lab coat.
   Hang it on the clothes line.   S.R.

5. After MRS. KENDAL change, ROSS overcoat taken off
   and hung.   S.R.

6. End of Picnic Scene, BISHOP back pants and shirt
   underdressed.
   Help underdress complete SNORK uniform with legs
   rolled up and secured by elastic garters and
   covered by BISHOP cassock.   S.R.

7. When completed, take GOMM's lab coat to S.L.   S.R.

8. End of Dream sequence, GOMM exits, throws Ross
   coat and cap and grey suit coat on two chairs.

Hold lab coat to put on.

Hand his comb and clip board from prop table.   S.L.

9. Gather Ross coat and cap, grey suitcoat and black cutaway from rack in change room and KENDAL shawl from chair and return promptly to S.R.   S.L.

10. Help GOMM into grey suitcoat.

Hang lab coat with black coat and MERRICK waistcoat on clothes line.

Hang MERRICK coat with velvet collar.   S.R.

11. Help BISHOP out of cassock, ecru collar and take to S.L., taking MERRICK coat at the same time.   S.R.

12. Help into BISHOP cassock, collar and stole.

Hang SNORK and take to S.R. and remove mourning band.   S.L.

13. Take BISHOP out of cassock, hang in change room with cravat.

Put BISHOP stole on clothes line and return to S.L.   S.R.

14. Wait for PROP MAN to get lab coats. Take to wardrobe to be pressed for the next performance.   S.R.

PROPERTY LIST

PROP PRESET

Stage Left

Damp mop in empty wooden bucket (ORDERLY)
Black folder with hand-written letter inside (Final Report) (GOMM)
Marbelized notebook with thin red medical book placed on top (TREVES)
Silver octagonal tray with doilie (ORDERLY)
    Decanter with sherry
    2 sherry glasses
1 financial times—pink (GOMM)
1 non-pictured newspaper—white (TREVES)
Silver-topped walking stick (LORD JOHN)
Wooden clipboard with papers (GOMM)
    Medical report on top
Wooden lunch tray with handles with bowl of cream of wheat (WILL)
    Plate with bread
Wood billy club (LONDON POLICE)
Green silk tablecloth (ORDERLY)
Crystal decanter with crystal goblet (ORDERLY)
Brown wood gift box with ivory-handled razor (MRS. KENDAL)
    Ivory-handled toothbrush inside
Gold-framed picture (GOMM)
Black and brown gift box (PRINCESS ALEXANDRA)
Small ring box (LORD JOHN)
Broom
Red Thomas Hardy book (ORDERLY)
Church S.L. wing piece (ORDERLY)
Church S.R. wing piece (ORDERLY)
Small tower church piece (ORDERLY)
Large tower church piece (ORDERLY)

Onstage—Act One
Curtains:
    U.R.—Pushed u.s. and untied
    CENTER—Pushed s.l. and tied

D.L.—Pushed u.s. and untied

Elephant Man—Set even with d.r. masking flat

Down Right:

Arm chair with blue leather seat in front of R. post #1

Down Left:

Arm chair with brown leather seat in front of L. post #1

White medical coat hung up of L. post #1 with small black
diary and pencil in r. pocket

Projection screen in up position

Left Center:

Strip lights on stage deck centered between L. post #1 and
L. post #2

Arm chair with brown leather set for Cellist set on stage
floor and R. of first left masking.

Music stand in front of arm chair.

Up Right:

Bed in u.s. position with pillow at head of bed

Grey blanket folded at the foot

Romeo and Juliet book at center

Merrick's photograph under pillow

Up Center:

Bath tub on spike in extreme u.c. position with natural
sponge on d.s. board, d.r. corner

Soap on d.s. board, d.l. corner

Blindhouse pamphlet on d.s. board, c.

White towel on d.s. board, d.l. corner covering soap

White medical smock, accordian folded, opening u.s.

Rag wet in drain of bathtub

Up Left:

Trunk at r. of L. post #3, lock facing d.s.

Table in u.s. position of track with leather folder
with four Merrick photographs papers secured to r. corner

Sketch pad in drawer with pencil inside cover

Right Center:

Gas petticock regulator up of R. post #2

Above:

Petticock rings turned to face left and right

Onstage—Act Two

Curtains:

U.R.—Pushed u.s. and tied

Center—Pushed s.l. and tied

D.L.—Pushed u.s. and tied

ELEPHANT MAN—Pushed off stage out of sight lines

Down Right:

Bench placed d.s. of R. post #1, perpendicular and on spike

Down Left:

Table in second d.s. position with church skeleton on top
S.L. window piece up of skeleton

Arm chair with brown leather seat placed next to L. post
#1 and flush to it

Grey gloves hung up of L. post #1 on hook

White medical coat hung up of L. post #1 on hook with
corset pamphlet set in l. pocket

Center:

Gift table on spike marks with church roof on top

Up Right:

Bed in extreme u.s. position with white coverlet over bed
White pillow sham
First act pillow underneath sham
Red Aeschylus book c. of bed
MERRICK's photograph under pillow
S.R. church window piece u.s. of pillow
Grey blanket made up with bed

Up Center:

Armchair covered with red velvet

Up Left:

Arm chair with blue leather seat, r. of L post #3

Stage Right

Wooden cane (TREVES)

Wooden bench (ORDERLY)

Silver tray with serviette (SNORK)
Blue plate with dark food
Silver goblet, secured to tray

Damp mop (WILL)

Portrait of Leopold on stand with rag (PINHEAD MANAGER)

Bible (BISHOP How)

U.S. end church piece (BISHOP How)

Steeple piece with cross (BISHOP How)

Visa with old business card (ROSS)

Change purse with coins inside (ROSS)

Felt cap with mask attached (ROSS)

Multi-colored letters, stapled at top (GOMM)
Carpet bag with ball of lavender yarn and wooden knitting
    needles (MRS. KENDAL)
    Financial Times inside
Instructions to TREVES office on 3 x 5 white paper
    (MRS. KENDAL)
Picnic basket with white linen cloth (MRS. KENDAL)
    2 wine glasses
    Wine bottle, corked, with wine
    Loaf of bread
    2 white napkins
    Bunch of violets on top of the basket
    Deck of cards on top of the basket
Silver Cigarette case with Sherman cigarettes cut to size inside
    (TREVES)
    2 stick matches stuck to inside
Silver tea tray with silver tea pot (ORDERLY)
    Silver sugarer
    Silver creamer
    Crystal bell
White Psalm book (BISHOP HOW)
2 Financial Times (ORDERLY)
Maroon umbrella with silver handle, wet (MRS. KENDAL)
Billy club, soft (BELGIAN POLICE)

PRESET FOR ACT TWO INTERMISSION CHANGE

Stage Left

Corset pamphlet
Gift table with church roof on top
Armchair covered with red velvet
Red Aeschylus book
Church skeleton
Church S.L. window piece
Church S.R. window piece
Decorative white bed spread
Decorative white pillow sham

Property Moves

1. Bring Gift Table (Square) from s.r. to s.l.
2. Move blue armchair from s.l. to d.s.r. in front of R. post
    #1.

3. Move brown armchair from top of table to d.s.l. in front of L. post #1.
4. Gas jets to "on."
5. Untie u.s.r. curtain.
6. Untie s.l. up and down curtain.
7. Tie on and off s.l. curtain.
8. Set Elephant Man Curtain 6" off right column edge.
9. Remove Act II coverlet and pillow sham from bed to armchair.
10. Fold blanket on bed to foot.
11. Place picture (head under pillow) under Act I pillow.
12. Check table drawer for drawing pad with pencil within.
13. Bring on bathtub and set to mark.
14. Arrange damp dry sponge, wash rag, blind pamphlet, gown and white towel on tub shelf.
15. Place trunk on mark, r. of L. post #3.
16. Remove bench to s.r.
17. Take wrung out mop, pail and push broom to s.l.
18. Take Romeo and Juliet from s.l. and place center of bed.
19. Place leather folder from s.r. to u.s.l. corner of table.
20. Place lab coat on hook up of L. post #1 on hook with diary and pencil in right pocket.
21. Set table off l. and off r. with props.
22. Set roof and wing and red leather book on gift table off l.

Intermission Property Moves

Stage Left	*Stage Right*
1. Bring on red velvet arm chair. Push tub upstage. Place arm chair on spike marks.	Take bed to upstage position.
2. Move bed linen from the chair to the bed.	Strike paper, pillows to blue arm chair.
3. Make up the bed with blankets, coverlet, two pillows and picture of MERRICK's mother.	
4. Take blue chair from U.S.R. to r. of L. post #3, even with post.	Get dolly for the tub.
5. Lift tub.	Put dolly under the tub.

6. Strike tub off UR ramp.

7. Tie u.r. curtain to R. post #3.

   Take lab coat from off stage r.

   Pick up gloves from up of R. post #3.

   Untie s.l. on and off curtain.
   Tie s.l. up and down curtain.

   Hang gloves and lab coat up of L. post #1.

8. Set bench perpendicular to the stage, spike marks on u.s. legs.

   Set tablo on ACT II spike marks.

   Place chair on d.r. of L. post #1.

   Strike sketch pad and pencil and put them in the drawer of table.

   Strike newspaper and "Romeo and Juliet" book to off left.

   Return with Corset pamphlet and put in the left hand pocket of lab coat.

9. Set gift table on center spike marks (d.s. legs) with roof piece and book preset.
   Place book c. of the bed.

   Set church skeleton on table.
   Place s.l. window piece u.s. of it.
   Place s.r. window piece u. of pillow on bed.

10. Check set.

    Check set.

Property Moves Stage Left

Act I

1. Take picture of Leopold, keeping picture and rag together. — Approx. 8:15
2. After KENDAL/TREVES scene take from TREVES the leather folder, diary and pencil and Blind pamphlet. — Approx. 8:45
3. Set out London Times (White newspaper). — Approx. 8:45
4. TREVES entrance, turn out all lights. — Approx. 8:55
5. With House Lights, turn on all lights. — Approx. 9:00

Act II

1. Turn off all lights, Top of Act.   Approx. 9:15
2. Light way for MRS. KENDAL.   Approx. 9:15
3. Immediately after Act start, hand crystal pitcher and goblet to ORDERLY, pitcher in right hand, goblet in left.   Aprrox. 9:15
4. Set notebook, medical book and clip board.   Approx. 9:40
5. As picnic basket and umbrella come off, open umbrella to dry and put shawl on chair for wardrobe. Wash and dry two glasses and wine bottles.   Approx. 9:50
6. Refill wine bottle with 2¼″ Tab, 9 drops of food coloring and water.   Approx. 9:50
7. Refriegrate wine bottle and return basket to prop box.   Approx. 9:50
8. During Death Scene, turn out all lights.   Approx. 10:10
9. During Blackout, strike tray.   Approx. 10:10
10. End of play, light actors off L#2.   Approx. 10:15

Property Moves Stage Right

Act I

1. Page Elephant Man Curtain R#1.   Approx. 8:10
2. Set Bench at R#2.   Approx. 8:20
   Catch Trunk at R#2 from ORDERLY.   Approx. 8:20
3. Hold Flashligtht end of Act I at UR for TREVES and MRS. KENDAL.   Approx. 9:00

Act II

1. Hand Silver Tray with Tea Service R#2 to ORDERLY.   Approx. 9:15
2. Set Wet Umbrella and Picnic Basket at R#2.   Approx. 9:40
   Catch Gift Table with Gifts at UR from ORDERLY.   Approx. 9:40
3. Take Clipboard to S.L.
4. Hand Silver Tray with Goblet to Ross.   Approx. 10:10
5. Hold Flashlight for MERRICK end of Death.   Approx. 10:15
6. Hold Flashlight for MRS. KENDAL end of show.   Approx. 10:17

PERSONAL PROPS

MERRICK:
  Knife
  Business cards
TREVES:
  Business cards
  Pencils
  Eyeglasses
  Wallet
  Coins
  Pocket watch
GOMM:
  Pince nez
  Watch fob chain
PINHEAD MANAGER:
  Glasses
LORD JOHN:
  Pocket Watch

SOUND PLOT—ACT ONE

Q#	DESCRIPTION	LENGTH	DECK	SPEAKERS	ACTION
A	Carriage and Street Noises	:40	A	SL & SR	5 pts, 8 ct.
A FADE	Carriage and Street Noises	:40	A	SL & SR	OUT, 12 ct.
A OUT	Carriage and Street Noises	:40	A	SL & SR	
B	Lecture Hall Voices	1:14	A	ALL HOUSE	
B OUT	Lecture Hall Voices	1:14	A	ALL HOUSE	OUT, 5 ct.
C	Audience Voice-over into Lecture Hall Voices	:43	A	BACK HOUSE	
C OUT	Audience Voice-over into Lecture Hall Voices	:43	A	BACK HOUSE	OUT, with D
D	Carnival Sounds	2:00	B	SL & SR	14 pts, 3 ct.
D FADE	Carnival Sounds	2:00	B	SL & SR	OUT, 8 ct.
D OUT	Carnival Sounds	2:00	B	SL & SR	
E	Hecklers	:45	A	SL	
E OUT	Hecklers	:45	A	SL	OUT, 6 ct.
F	Boat Horns, Wharf Sounds, Clanging Bells	1:00	A	SR	
F FADE	Boat Horns, Wharf Sounds, Clanging Bells	1:00	A	SR	11 pts, 3 ct.
F OUT	Boat Horns, Wharf Sounds, Clanging Bells	1:00	A	SR	OUT, with G